What was the date today? Here, time didn't pass in days and years. I wouldn't be surprised if spring arrived and slid straight into summer, if I looked at a clear lake and saw an old woman in my reflection.

Praise for *Hunger*

'An instant cult classic. You have to read it.'
Harper's Bazaar

'A feast for the literary senses.'
Anton Hur, translator of *Cursed Bunny*

'Mesmerising. Inject it into my veins again.'
Irenosen Okojie, author of *Butterfly Fish*

'A novella as slender as it is profound. I was enraptured.'
Ling Ling Huang, author of *Natural Beauty*

'A gutting, unforgettable ode to doomed love.
Which is to say, all love.'
Henry Hoke, author of *Open Throat*

'*Hunger* cuts to the heart. Read at your peril.'
Frances Cha, author of *If I Had Your Face*

'It glistens with raw and primal romance.
I could not put it down.'
Jade Song, author of *Chlorin*e

'I savoured every word. A novel of remarkable depth.'
Ayesha Manazir Siddiqi, author of *The Centre*

brazen

First Edition

First published in Great Britain in 2021 by Honford Star as *To the Warm Horizon*
This edition published in Great Britain in 2026 by Brazen, an imprint of
Octopus Publishing Group Ltd
Carmelite House
50 Victoria Embankment
London EC4Y 0DZ
www.octopusbooks.co.uk

An Hachette UK Company
www.hachette.co.uk

The authorised representative in the EEA is Hachette Ireland,
8 Castlecourt Centre, Dublin 15, D15 XTP3, Ireland (email: info@hbgi.ie)

Distributed in the US by Hachette Book Group
1290 Avenue of the Americas, 4th and 5th Floors
New York, NY 10104

Distributed in Canada by Canadian Manda Group
664 Annette St., Toronto, Ontario, Canada M6S 2C8

Trade Paperback ISBN: 978-1-84091-986-8
eISBN: 978-1-84091-989-9

A CIP catalogue record for this book is available from the British Library.

Typeset in 10.5/17.5pt Farnham Text by Six Red Marbles UK, Thetford, Norfolk

Printed and bound in Great Britain

1 3 5 7 9 10 8 6 4 2

This FSC® label means that materials used for the product have been responsibly sourced.

Contents

Prologue

Ryu

Have you heard of Korea?

Is Korea still where it used to be?

I was born in Korea. That's where I met Dan and gave birth to Haerim and Haemin.

That was a long time ago.

Haemin now lives in Warsaw. His wife recently gave birth to their fourth child. They named her Bona. They say she's as small as Haemin's head. I will never see that small, precious, precarious bundle of life. Never get to touch her, hold her, kiss her.

Haerim died when she was eleven years old. We abandoned Korea because she died. When we left, I abandoned explanation as well. Haemin was seven then, the age of endless questions. Haemin couldn't understand why his parents would leave behind his bicycle, his computer and his sister's room. I couldn't explain. I couldn't say, *Some of us have to survive.*

I was lying in bed when I heard the midnight news. It was a Monday. A strange virus spreading in some distant country, mutating with every new vaccine. Exhausted, I found myself calculating monthly expenses – birthdays, funerals, weddings – while the newsreader explained that there was no way of knowing what to look out for because the infection process was still unknown. By the next day, talk of the virus filled every street. *It'll pass soon,* we told ourselves. *The disaster is far away. Modern medicine will protect us. The government will protect us.* Even as death tolls surged in the Americas, we worried about the cost of living, retirement, our children's education. Then the call came. Haerim was dead. Less than an hour after reaching the hospital. She'd overslept that morning. After washing her face and tying her hair back, she complained her forehead felt hot. She mumbled something about wanting a Bulgogi Whopper as she shouldered her school bag – soft words to herself, like chanting an old wish. I handed her a five thousand won note and told her to buy one after school. She hugged me tight around my waist, rubbed her head against my chest. 'I'll get you medicine on my way home from work,' I said. My last words to her.

The official death toll that day, in Korea alone, was over a hundred thousand. It increased nearly fivefold the next day. We claimed Haerim's body from the hospital and buried her in the hills behind our neighbourhood. We dug into the earth without shedding a single tear. The parting had struck like lightning. We knew nothing of death. Only as we lowered her body into the pit and began covering it with dirt did I understand: I was dumping Haerim into the ice-cold earth.

Shrieking, I jumped into the grave and embraced her. I wanted to hold her and be buried with her. She looked like she didn't know she was dead. As she lay there on the frozen earth, she looked like she was waiting for class to end so she could eat her burger. I covered her with dirt, having failed to leave her favourite burger by her side.

Mass bankruptcy brought disaster worse than disease: robberies, smuggling, human trafficking, murder, violence, cults. Male mortality rates soared. Rumours spread that eating children's livers could cure the infected. Governments collapsed. Public order crumbled. We could neither stay nor leave.

Still, some tried to stay. Those who believed it would be the same anywhere. Those who wouldn't abandon what remained of their lives, memories without flesh or bone. Those who said if they must die, let it be at home. Like noble heroes, like warriors laying down their weapons, they held their ground. I abandoned everyone except Dan and Haemin. My father. My sister and her family. Old friends. Did they think they abandoned me, too? We'd promised we would reunite somewhere, someday, even after wronging each other and going our separate ways. That was our wide-eyed delusion.

When we reached Vladivostok, having abandoned everything and endured so much, confusion descended upon us once more. Where to go now? Was there a place for us here? But the land was vast. We could keep moving. Wander to avoid the virus and the lawless bandits. Watch the sunset from somewhere different each day – today here, tomorrow there, never the same place twice. Always fleeing the present. What drove us forward pierced through solid earth, soared like the sun, shone on us daily. Everyone in that land believed in God. God's purpose, God's grace, God's gifts from Heaven, God watching over us, God knows all . . . I believed in their God and feared Him. The landscape – stretching menacing and senseless as if to say, *I have no use for you humans* – made me fear Him more.

Then there was Dori, glaring at me as she held her little sister close in a small chapel near Ulan-Ude. I had thrust Haemin into her arms and slammed the doors shut. The first time I'd trusted my child with someone on Russian soil. Dori held Haemin like her own sister and crouched in the corner. After the bandits had passed, I opened the doors. Dori was muttering to herself.

—God is punishing us. The god of this land is telling us to leave.

When we met again in Tomsk, Dori had lost her fear of God. She'd stopped believing in any of it. Without faith, there was no reason to curse Him either. I was frightened by the change in her, but I wanted so badly to trust who she'd become.

*

I am now over seventy years old – no, eighty? I'm not sure. I have lived too long. Relative to my years, the two or so months I spent in Russia would at most amount to one sheep in a herd of a hundred. Yet that sheep remains vivid. Not a day passes that I don't remember you all.

God no longer punishes me. He's lost interest. I've survived this long through His indifference. If only I could have shared this wretched life with my daughter.

Do you know Korea?

Is Korea still there?

There was a time when I wandered around Russia, fleeing the disaster that shrouded the world. I was thirty-nine then.

Everything Happened at Once

Dori

I think about one thing: never leave Joy behind. So I must survive no matter what. I must do my part as someone still alive. This imperative is a *Da Capo* without a *Fine*, a prayer I dedicate to myself. As Mum was dying, she asked Dad to look after us. As Dad was dying, he asked me to look after Joy. Like a secret key in some legend, Joy was handed down from Mum to Dad, from Dad to me. What could I ask of Joy in my dying moment? *I love you*. I will ask her to look after love. Joy, with my love handed down to her, will survive somehow. With love in her arms, she'll dash towards the end of the world.

'It's fine,' our parents kept reassuring us. Humans were intelligent and persistent, they said. Those smart people would find a solution; we just had to wait. I believed the opposite. The world would certainly be upended. Human determination would turn crisis into despair. Smart people wouldn't find solutions but create bigger disasters. I needed a different approach than my parents'. The day Dad died, I packed my bags immediately. As light as possible. Only what I could carry on the run. I took Joy by the hand and headed straight to Incheon harbour. I wasn't sure if there'd be a ship running under such circumstances, but there was. The problem was just that the tickets were unbelievably expensive. People who see opportunity in disaster, who don't starve or run even in disaster – they must belong to a world somewhere beyond the afterlife. To ride on the boat, I had to offer up as much gold and diamonds as they wanted. A gold ring wasn't even enough to cop a pack of gum. However, in exchange for my parents, God gave me the talent of stealing. I came to know something much better than ever before: what I needed, where it was. Like a rat, I burrowed into the bedlam of screaming, brawling, milling people and stole two tickets. Tickets to Qingdao. There, I stole another pair of tickets. We travelled all the way to Ulan-Ude that way. What happened to the people I robbed? It wasn't just tickets or money but their lives I stole. I deserved their hatred.

I got caught in Ulan-Ude. Joy and I ran. She's fast – so fast I can't keep up. But she can't run as fast as she wants because she holds my hand. I'm the millstone around her neck. Without me, Joy could run to the continent's end without cars or trains, without getting tired. She could run and run until she took flight like a bird. I tried keeping up as she dragged me forward but had to let go. Joy stopped like a switched-off toy. The small angel turned back, her guileless eyes finding mine. I'm why Joy can't run. Dad's request was wrong. Instead of asking me to look after Joy, he should've told her to keep running even if her sister lets go. My letting go should be her cue to run faster.

*

Russia also had its share of crazy bastards hunting children's livers. The rumour was that eating a girl's liver worked better than eating a boy's. If only I were a magician. If only I could hide Joy away in my pocket like turning a handkerchief into a rose or making a pigeon disappear inside a top hat . . . We had to avoid places with too many people, but places without people were also places without food. Mountain paths meant wild animals. We had to beware of long-starved dogs as well. Cities and villages occasionally appeared as we walked like cattle or horses along railroad tracks. The remaining villagers kept their distance. They feared the people on the road, and the people on the road feared them. A misread gesture could get someone killed. In abandoned cities, we scavenged for food and clothes. Whenever wind and snow besieged us on barren plains, I cursed my body for feeling so much. God, who they say exists only in words and light, probably doesn't know hunger or frostbite. He can't be omniscient. But that's how He stays immortal. If only we could understand each other. I wanted to ask someone, anyone: When does winter end on this land? Does spring arrive in Russia, too?

Last spring.

I was listening to a late-night radio show. Bundled up in a blanket, my hands wrapped around a warm mug of coffee. The rain suddenly began to pour just past two in the morning. The thought of all the white flowers wilting made me feel a little mournful yet relieved. I turned down the radio to listen to the rain.

It was after my midterms. I spent that night brooding over my English test scores, worrying if I would ever find a job in my desired field, tossing and turning in bed with a slight headache. I woke to brilliant sunlight quietly lapping away last night's rain. I had a dream back then: to host my own late-night radio show. To spend my dawns in a small studio.

Back then, death was distant while the reality in front of me was both harsh and tedious. My parents had been paying off their loans for over a decade, I had my own loans to take care of, and Joy was lonely without friends. Even in happy moments, a vague melancholy clung to me like body odour, impossible to wash off. There was a fog separating me from the world, and I gave vague answers to anyone who asked me anything. But we had a heated floor that kept us warm and a roof that sheltered us from rain and snow. If I felt scared and repulsed by the world, I could close my bedroom door and hide under my desk and listen to music. Water and kimchi were in the fridge, rice in the rice cooker, and instant ramen in the cupboard. I could turn on the light. I could shower with warm water. I could buy and drink beer from the convenience store, where a quick scan of the barcode would show the price. I could stand still on the side of a road and look at the passersby without hatred or fear. I could just look at them.

If nothing had happened, nothing would've happened.

We would've continued not owning the house we lived in. Started paying off another loan as soon as we were done with one. Occasionally pushed death aside with the words, *I'm so exhausted I could die.* Whittled our own lives away, silently and ever so calmly.

—We're leaving before spring.

A woman, the one who shoved her son into my arms, said this to me while we were hiding in the oratory. She had a husband and a car. She didn't drive off right away, even after stashing her son in the backseat. She seemed afraid to leave Joy and me behind on the road. Had I not been Korean and with Joy, the woman wouldn't have hesitated to leave. She certainly wouldn't have trusted me with her son. I'd happened to spot her car while walking; had there been no one inside, I would've stolen everything I could find. Even down to their last tin of food.

We walked away first while she hesitated. Behind us, I heard the car door open and shut. The woman slowly backed up next to me. She lowered her window and told me to take anything we needed from the backseat. It was in return for keeping her son safe, she said. Blankets, clothes, water bottles, tinned goods and dry foods crowded the backseat. I accidentally made eye contact with the woman's husband while looking over those items. His eyes looked dim. Like he'd lost something important. Despite being with his wife and son, despite riding in a car loaded with food and water, the man was weary. I took two tins of tuna and stepped away from the car. Even then, the woman did not leave. I approached the car again to grab two packets of powdered soup and two tins of beans. She scooped out a handful of sweets from a black bag and held them out to me. Only after I accepted the sweets did the car drive away. Its wheels turned slowly at first, then accelerated soon enough.

I put these items in my rucksack and a boiled sweet in Joy's mouth. Her frayed shoes, the soles flapping from wear, caught my eye. Walking would become even more excruciating by night. I longed for a nice, long bath. Would it be better if it were summer? Then we could at least bathe in a lake. We could sleep without walls or ceilings. Hope might not exist on a continent I had to reach on foot, but in time itself. A bright, warm season that arrives after the Earth completes its orbit. Perhaps all we can do is survive and welcome that season. Winter will come again, I'm sure. Like time, hope is something that comes and goes, never staying. Where were they going? Did they lose their family too?

Joy glanced up at me and asked,

—Where are those people going?

—I don't know.

—Where are *we* going?

—We're . . . looking for summer.

—Where's summer?

I pointed to the sun.

—There, the horizon. Where the sun sets.

Rolling the sweet in her mouth, Joy held my hand tight.

We reached a dreary and desolate village, empty except for traces of former lives. I eyed an old house near the train tracks. No glass in the windows, the door off its hinges. It looked dark and deep inside. I threw several rocks through the window and waited for a while, but there was no sign of life. Rummaging around the area, I scraped together some things that looked flammable. As soon as we stepped into the house, I made a fire, opened up a tin of tuna and split it with Joy. Night came quickly. Joy fell asleep with her body tightly curled up. I took out the sleeping bag and shook her awake. Barely conscious, she managed to crawl inside the sleeping bag.

Pulling a blanket over me, I thought only about our shoes: *If I had a car, I wouldn't have to worry about shoes. If not a car, a motorcycle. No. Even if I had something like that, petrol would be a problem. I saw someone get shot while stealing petrol. A bike then. Yes, I should find a bike . . . But even if I find one, or a car with enough petrol, where would I go? If I reached the end of the world, could I avoid death? Is it really up to us to leave or stay? Where could I go to find hope?* I tried to stick to the shoes, but my thoughts kept spinning out of control, wearing me down. The distant sound of a train got closer and closer, and a sharp pain shot through my body. *If only I could get on a train. If only*

I could get inside that solid, hulking thing and get just a little farther away from this goddamn cold. The house shook slightly. Joy stirred in her sleep. *We'll walk into the village once it gets darker out. We have to find shoes tonight.* With that thought, I must've dozed off.

I opened my eyes. The fire had gone out. I heard murmuring. Korean. It sounded like more than a couple of people. It still looked dark outside. I woke Joy and took a peek. Two box vans were parked in the vegetable garden. I counted more than ten people. Several of them waved their torches into the house. I hid in the farthest corner of the room with Joy in my arms. People moved about, lighting a fire and heating up their food. They made hot water from the snow and washed their hands and faces. The smell of grilled meat wafted in. I gagged and held Joy close to my chest. So she wouldn't be able to smell anything. So she wouldn't see anything. With only a wall separating us, these people ate and drank and spoke in Korean. They called each other honey, you, sir.

—Jina. Jina.

A man spoke in a low but clear voice.

—It's dangerous. Don't go off on your own.

This Jina didn't seem to heed the man. The man called after Jina several more times. Along with a beam of torchlight, a small head suddenly popped through the window. A little later I heard light, quick footsteps move towards the missing door. I hid Joy behind my back and took out my jackknife.

The torchlight that had suddenly appeared out of the black empty space shone on me.

—Jina, get back here. Don't go just anywhere. I'm telling you, it's dangerous.

The person at the window lowered their torch, then leaned outside.

—Fine! I'm coming, I'm coming.

With this, Jina turned away from the window and looked at me without a word. I held the jackknife up to my chest. She did not come any closer. She laid down the torch, pointing the light at herself. With her face and body totally bundled up in bulky winter clothes, I could only make out a pair of eyes and a nose under a hat. After staring at me intently, Jina suddenly took off her woolly hat and revealed more of herself. Her hair was a dark blood-red. I recoiled in surprise. Joy squirmed and stuck her head out from behind me.

—Oh.

Jina broke the silence.

—I see there's a little kid too.

She drew a little closer.

—Is she your little sister?

She asked without hesitation, as if chatting with a friend.

—Not your daughter, obviously . . .

She murmured as if thinking out loud, combing through her dishevelled hair with her fingers.

—Is it just you and the kiddo?

Jina did not put her guard up with me.

—You're from Korea, right?

I, on the other hand, did not let my guard down. Jina scratched her cheek, looking at me as I said nothing in response.

—A-im peurom Koria.

English, suddenly.

—Wheo al yu peurom?

I sensed a slight Gyeongsang accent.

—Naiseu tu mit yu.

She took another step towards me and extended her hand.

—If it's not that either . . . *Hajimemashite.*

Greeting me in Japanese, Jina quietly gazed at me for a moment, fixed her hat and switched back to Korean.

—Don't worry. We're not bad people. No one's infected, and we don't eat kid liver. We're going to spend the night right outside and leave in the morning . . . I won't tell anyone that I saw you here.

With a faint smile, Jina slowly backed away and out of sight. The light faded, and the air fell dark again. I felt like I had dreamed with my eyes open. My heart was pounding hard. Not because I was afraid . . . No, I was afraid. No, it wasn't that I was afraid . . . I was afraid.

Joy tugged at my sleeve.

—Are we leaving now?

I nodded, then shook my head. I signed back.

—Let's stay here tonight.

Sitting upright, I kept dozing off. Between my catnaps,

the view outside the window gradually deepened into black-blue. I ended up lying on my side. My consciousness poured into a black pit as if I were plunging into hell. Even in my sleep, I remembered Jina's English and chuckled. It woke me. A campfire was blazing. I sat up. Jina held out a small cup.

—Coffee.

She placed the cup in my hand. Half convinced I was still asleep, I stared at the pure white steam blooming and rising from the black liquid. As I held the cup, Jina wrapped her hand around mine, tipping the cup to her own lips. Then, without letting go of my hand, she tipped the cup to my lips. My lips were gently wetted by the black liquid. It was real coffee. Real. Coffee. I sipped it sweetly. The warmth spread through me, waking every cell in my body. I continued taking little sips without lifting my lips from the cup.

—Your shoes are a mess.

Jina muttered, patting my shoes. I kept thinking about her blood-red hair. Had I imagined it? I was thinking about how much I wanted to take off that woolly hat to see if I'd dreamed it all up, just thinking about it, when my hand tugged at her hat, exposing her red hair.

—Agh . . . My hair's probably super gross and oily and matted down . . .

She muttered again as she ran her fingers through her hair, but she didn't show any sign of embarrassment.

—You're also from Korea, right?

She warmed her hands by the fire.

—What should I call you?

I was flustered.

—You can call me Jina.

Jina came into focus, right before my eyes. Hers were the colour of ash. She rubbed her nose.

—By the way, where're you going? Have you decided?

My eyes couldn't lie, and Jina kept trying to meet them. I lowered my head and drank the coffee. Jina laid her hand on mine and pressed down a little. As if saying, *Look at me,* so I looked up.

—Do you want to go with me?

Jina, with those grey eyes and that red hair.

—Let's go together.

I knew. What I needed. Where it was.

Jina

The early risers filled the air with voices and clatter. I stood outside the window and waved Dori over. She held Joy's hand as they walked up to me. I pointed to each person, explaining who was who, then locked eyes with Dad. He didn't even flinch when he saw Dori. He was impossible to surprise. In Korea, my extended family had all lived in the same neighbourhood. There used to be more than fifty of us. Of that fifty, we lost at least thirty in a matter of two days. Even then, Dad never panicked. My aunt who lost her parents and her children hanged herself. My uncle who lost his wife and his children jumped from his apartment building. My dad, who lost his parents, his wife and his siblings, declared with terrifying calm that no one else would die. Not on his watch. He started collecting gold and diamonds from anyone who'd give them up, selling off every car from his used import dealership. All except two big, sturdy box vans. He packed our surviving relatives into those box vans with whatever supplies we could carry, and we escaped Korea.

People always told me I took after my dad. I heard it so

much I believed them. Now I see things differently. I don't actually resemble him – I just grew up being told I did, which made me become like him.

I told Dad I wanted to take Dori and Joy with us. He didn't hesitate.

—This is the last time.

That was all he said.

—After this, no one else.

He made sure I understood.

—Once you get in, you'll pay for the ride.

He stared directly at Dori.

—If you've got a gun, hand it over now.

Without a word, Dori opened her rucksack and let Dad rifle through it. He patted down both her and Joy. When he found a jackknife in Dori's pocket, he burst out laughing.

—What are you going to do with this thing?

He kept that condescending smirk as he mimed opening a tin with her knife. But when Dori mentioned she'd escaped Korea and walked from Ulan-Ude with Joy, he went quiet.

—Without help?

Dad studied Dori's blank expression.

—Without killing anyone?

Dori said nothing. Joy looked scared but managed a small smile when our eyes met.

—How long did that take?

—I didn't count the days.

— . . . Fair enough.

Dad pocketed the jackknife. Dori asked for it back.

—Too dangerous.

—That tiny thing that can barely open a tin?

—Doesn't matter. No.

—Please give it back.

—When I can trust you.

—There's no need for that. Please give it back now.

—What's that supposed to mean?

—You don't need to trust me. I'm not planning to trust you either.

Dad played with the knife, staring at her. She never looked away.

—I suppose that's more honest than asking me to trust you.

He handed it back.

—You follow my orders from now on. Step out of line, and you're gone. Don't expect us to treat you like family.

Several relatives complained when they heard Dad's decision. How many more strays were we going to pick up? There wasn't enough food to go around. Who were these kids really? What if they stole from us? What if the little girl made us targets? But no one dared oppose him.

I locked eyes with Geonji. He was leaning against a tyre, combing his hair over his forehead, making a serious face. The only one among us who wasn't family. He, too, had come with us because of me. We'd been neighbours for over a decade; he spent more time at our house than his own. He was always getting beaten up, both at home and at school. Mum even marched into school to confront his teacher, then went round to every parent whose kid hit Geonji. But she couldn't fight his dad – that might've got her killed.

After Geonji's mum fell ill and died, his dad drunkenly tried to kill Geonji and himself. Geonji hid in our shed and wouldn't come out, even after his dad had died. I couldn't help him as he starved for days in that dark shed. Recalling those days . . . time collapses on itself. I can't recall the events in order . . . no, there is no order. Everything happened at once. Geonji's dad, my mum, my relatives, our neighbours – all dead in an instant. The sun still came up even when I didn't sleep. I couldn't breathe, but I didn't die. I was in a state of consciousness where I couldn't tell whether what I was seeing and hearing were nightmares or reality. Looking at a burning building, I wondered if it was something I'd done. Looking at the dead, I trembled with fear, unsure if I'd killed them. The world spun on in a macabre dance. A distorted melody sounded from every direction. I didn't speak, but curses leaked out anyway. I didn't cry, but tears streamed down my face. When I climbed into the box van to leave, I locked eyes with Geonji watching from behind the shed door. Only then did I realise that he was still alive. I sprinted over and grabbed his hand. He clung to the door and refused to come out. Even when I pulled hard enough to lose my balance, he wouldn't budge. Dad jumped out, threw me over his shoulder and tossed me into the cargo hold. I screamed and ran straight back to Geonji. If they wanted me, they had to take him too. My family didn't like it – Geonji wasn't blood. But he held his head high. Out here, he was braver than he'd ever been in Korea.

The other day, Geonji spoke to me with a dazed look on his face.

—I remembered this time I was watching football at the salon, some match against Qatar. This old guy getting his hair cut was watching too, getting all worked up, cursing at the screen. Then he goes, 'They're such crap, it's like they're playing with their feet!'

I waited for the punchline.

—He was mad that they were playing *football* with their *feet*.

Only then did I get it and burst out laughing.

—So the lady was like, 'They're supposed to kick the ball with their feet. What do you want them to do, run their mouths like somebody over here?'

I could picture it so clearly I giggled, then caught myself. My relatives were giving us icy stares.

We who'd lost everything weren't allowed to laugh.

We'd left our humour behind in our hometown.

The older folks didn't speak unless absolutely necessary. Words were like buckets drawing from a well of pain; the longer they talked, the more bitterness spilled over. Even without raising their voices or hurling insults, conversations froze to a halt. Self-hatred and guilt had settled deep in their eyes and voices. The belief that surviving was sinful, that continuing to evade death was even worse, that we were all damned. I understood. Our tragedy had made us this way. Death had us pinned down. We couldn't escape memory, too exhausted to imagine any future. That's exactly why I refused to resemble misfortune. I didn't want to despise life. I didn't understand death or life yet, but at the very least, I wouldn't treat either as some kind of fluke or punishment. Because if I did, I couldn't cope with Mum's death or my own survival.

—It's probably wrong to think this way, but . . .

One night, Geonji confessed. He said sometimes he actually felt relieved living like this. No school, no father, everyone equally screwed. At least now he didn't think about wanting to die. He felt like he could handle himself now if anyone tried, if he ever went back to Korea and attended school again — but he didn't want to find out.

—So you don't want to go back?

—Nothing good there anymore. Your mum's gone too.

—Where do you want to go instead?

—I've been thinking about that constantly, and . . .

Geonji was planning for the future. The same kid who used to say, 'Scum like me should just drop dead.'

— . . . an ocean that's warm year-round would be nice.

He said even if it took forever, he'd keep moving until he found a place like that. Build a house by the beach, swim in the ocean, catch fish, pick sweet berries and share them with someone he loved. Geonji had a dream. Something he'd never had in Korea, born after disaster.

—Do *you* want to go back to Korea?

I'd assumed I'd return once things settled down. How naive. What was waiting for us in Korea? Nothing. Same as here. No – here we had family. We had an endless road stretching ahead, a tomorrow we couldn't predict. Back in Korea, I'd wanted to become a fashion designer, but dreams like that were useless now. *A warm ocean where I can build a house and swim and catch fish and* . . . I had to dream those dreams instead. Because that kind of ocean had to exist somewhere, even if fashion designers didn't. Because no matter how much time passes, even if humans go extinct, the ocean would still be there.

—Or do you want to come with me?

His eyes shone with determination, something I'd never seen in him before. To dream. To share that dream. For Geonji, a dream was something untouched and new, like a first love he could embrace wholly without weighing the risks, having never known failure. I tried imagining the warm ocean of a world in ruins. The image felt empty and forlorn, as hollow as the silence after a symphony ends.

*

I tried to give Dori my shoes, but she wouldn't take them. She refused even the food I'd set aside for her. Dori wouldn't touch anything from the box van. She always sat on the outermost edge where she could open the door and jump out at any moment, curled up in her corner as if she couldn't see or hear anything. Like a bundle of blankets. One of my aunts said, 'At least she knows her place.' My uncle's wife was harsher: 'That girl is too cold. When an adult asks her a question, she should at least respond.' Even as my relatives made these remarks, Dori never broke her silence or changed her blank expression. She sat motionless as a doll, breathing soundlessly, only seeming human when she looked at Joy. So I became a doll too, sitting across from them, watching Dori all day.

Everything about Dori was delicate and long – her eyes, her nose, her lips, even her ears. Her petite frame looked like a sapling you'd plant on Arbor Day. If we ever grew closer, I wanted to untangle the hair that spilled from her woolly hat. I wanted to comb it, braid it, maybe cut it to her shoulders. I wanted to tell her she was cute. How old was she? Where had she lived? What had she done for a living? What had happened to her parents? What had her life been like in Korea? I didn't ask. I just watched her, letting imaginary conversations play out between us in the back of that bumpy box van. Maybe it was better not knowing. I didn't know Dori's wounds, and she didn't know mine. Maybe that's why we could see each other just as we were in that moment. We could even write a new story of our own.

After speeding down a two-lane motorway all day, we drove into a city in ruins. Like everywhere else we'd passed, it was buried in snow and darkness. I occasionally spotted people but couldn't tell if they were locals or other drifters. The streets looked bleak and dirty, every shop showing signs of looting. We decided to fix the car and spend the night.

Even when my family gathered for dinner, Dori and Joy sat far from us, eating bits of tinned food and sipping bottled water from their bags. Then they disappeared. I worried they had left for good, but they returned before dark. Dori was wearing different shoes – not new, but no more holes. Joy's shoes were different too. Dori built a small fire, using the building near our box van as a windbreak, and laid out their sleeping bags. Watching her do this made me angry. I'd spent the whole day wound up, worrying about where she was, what she'd eaten, how she was feeling.

—Sleep in the car instead. If you're uncomfortable around the older folks, just stay with me.

Dori tucked a blanket over Joy and checked the fire.

—I'm telling you, even if something bad happens, you're safest with me.

Dori shook her head.

—There's nowhere safe.

—Right. So let's stay together.

—I'm fine out here.

—Well, I'm not fine with that.

—Don't worry about me.

—How can I not? I'm the one who put you in this car.

Dori was quiet for a moment.

— . . . I really do appreciate it.

She spoke slowly.

—I'm being careful for a reason. Everyone's lost someone. They probably don't like a stranger showing up and acting like she's family. *Why did my boy die, and why is she alive? Why is she eating food he should've eaten?* That's how they look at me . . .

—Fine. Suit yourself.

Because I couldn't tell Dori she had it all wrong, because I couldn't hate her for saying what she said, because I couldn't argue any longer, I was about to turn around when Dori caught my hand and immediately let go. A small box sat in my palm, like magic. I opened the box. Lipstick. Glossy and rose-scented.

—Where did you get this?

I murmured, unable to take my eyes off the tube. Dori gestured at my hair.

—I thought it'd go well together.

I put it on straight away. With my lips so dry and chapped, it didn't glide on like before, but I felt better just breathing in the sweet rose scent. Dori cleaned up my lip line with her finger. I tried to put it on her as well, but she dodged and refused.

Giddy, I bounced around Dori like a filly, then brought over my sleeping bag and blanket from the box van.

—Didn't you say you didn't want to sleep in the car? I can sleep here, then.

—Your dad won't like that.

—Doesn't matter.

—If your dad doesn't like me, then I can't ride in his car.

—Come lie down.

Dori refused to listen, and I refused right back. I clutched the lipstick, lay on my side and stared at her. The moment she gave it to me, I realised how desperately I'd wanted it. On this desolate, frozen stretch of land – this endless, endless road – surrounded by people worn down by tragedy and despair, I'd been craving exactly this kind of thing. Not something to eat or wear for survival, but something that made me feel like myself. Something I couldn't live without, like jokes and laughter, despite everyone's disapproving looks. Suddenly, regret struck me. When we fled Korea, I'd only grabbed a few photos of Mum as keepsakes. I should have taken more things like this lipstick: Mum's makeup, her scarves, her pyjamas, things that carried her scent and touch.

Mum's hair salon had been my personal playground. I'd played with brushes, wigs and makeup there since I was very young. It always smelled wonderful. The fridge never ran out of yogurt, and there were always sachets of instant coffee and snacks on the old table by the sofa. Pastries, rice crackers or boiled sweet potatoes – Mum didn't have to prepare any of it because the neighbourhood ladies always brought things over. They'd bring food to share, chat for hours and hours, then suddenly rush out of the salon saying, 'Oh my, look at the time!' The regulars were like sparrows, carrying all sorts of fun stories in their beaks.

The summer I turned fifteen, I completely fried the ends of my hair messing about with the straightening iron. That's when Mum cut my hair short. I loved how I looked in the mirror. Since Mum had already shaped it, I just had to trim it occasionally with the salon scissors. Easy as cutting grass. I even cut Geonji's hair once. He went mental when I finished, but I convinced him it looked cool and unique. The next day he came home from school furious again. Mum also taught me about makeup. She had this gift for finding colours that suited my skin. She loved beautiful things, was beautiful herself, and knew how to spot beauty everywhere. Because I was a girl, Grandfather let Mum and Dad choose my name. Mum decided instantly. I love my name – it was her first gift to me. Even when I fought with friends, hearing them say my name would melt the anger right out of me. I'd think, *How can this stupid grudge matter?*

—Jina.

Dori called my name, stroking my cheek.

—Please. Go sleep in the car.

I shook my head, still thick with sleep.

—We have to stay together. That's the only way we'll be safe.

I don't know if I said that before I fell asleep or while dreaming. I'm not even sure whether I said it or Dori did. When I opened my eyes in the morning, only those words remained clear. Tattooed across my heart like a motto only I knew.

Dori

The road continued.

Snow blanketing the earth hardened into ice, as if taunting the clear skies and blinding sunlight.

We couldn't get news on the road - how far the virus had spread, how many humans remained, how many cities lay destroyed across the world. The cold and devastation before us became our only reality, our entire world. Those who left ahead of us grew farther away. No one ever returned.

Joy and I had to decide in advance: How long would we continue travelling with these people?

I didn't want to open up foolishly and grow weak, to agonise over the dead every time warmth touched my heart. When I left Korea, I told myself I would only keep Joy by my side. So I wouldn't break down, no matter who died. So I wouldn't resent anyone, even if I died.

Every morning, Joy asked the same question.

—When are we leaving?

I extended my thumbs and index fingers, shaking them up and down twice. *Always.* She nodded, understanding.

Jina's father paid more attention to petrol than food. He stacked ten petrol drums in each box van and filled them at every opportunity. Though petrol stations were usually empty, we occasionally found one with fuel. Those places were already occupied by rough, unsavoury people. To get petrol from them, we had to give them all the gold and diamonds they wanted. Some even demanded young women. Whenever Jina's father stopped the box vans by the roadside, I placed a blanket over Joy and clutched the jackknife in my pocket. Jina always got out first to tell us what was happening outside. Though she said multiple times, 'Don't worry, we'll never sell you two,' it was better to forget such promises the moment you heard them.

Crime spread like the virus. It had been the same in Korea. At first, everyone worried mainly about getting sick. They thought if they avoided going outside, kept their distance and stayed home, they'd be safe. As time passed, more people died in muggings and arson attacks. A bizarre new religion promoting murder as repentance became popular. When Mum lay dying, Dad, Joy and I held her cold hands and cried together. When Dad lay dying, Joy and I had to hide in the boiler room, holding our breath. Robbers crashed into our house like a tank, slashed Dad's body, looted everything remotely useful. When Joy and I crawled out to hold his hand, Dad was still alive, soaked in blood. He stopped breathing only after seeing we were safe.

Though I had lived it, it didn't feel like the past. It felt like the future – a sensation I would experience perpetually in the days to come.

It snowed heavily for three days. We stayed in a bleak village near the frozen river, waiting for it to stop. A small village with fewer than thirty houses, every one of them abandoned. Many had been torched or raided. After looking for a decent place to rest, Jina and I came across a house with a stable. She looked around and muttered.

—There must've been horses.

She kicked a frozen lump of dirt tangled in the hay.

—Looks like horse dung.

—How do you know that?

—We had a neighbour who raised horses.

It sounded like a fairytale. I imagined Jina riding through a field.

—No, I never rode one myself. But I often went to see them because they were so beautiful.

—Beautiful?

—Yeah, their eyes were like black pearls, their manes like silk. I've never seen real black pearls, but no jewel could be prettier than those horses' eyes. Cows are beautiful too. I'd be mesmerised looking into their eyes and lose track of time.

Sometimes the owner let me touch them, and in winter they were so warm that I wanted to climb on one's back, hug it, and feel its warmth against my stomach.

—Did you live in a rich neighbourhood?

—No, the countryside. You know, cows and pigs and chickens.

The only animals I saw as a kid were dogs, cats, goldfish, sparrows and pigeons. I thought about it, but that was really all. Cows, pigs, chickens – I only saw them in pictures, videos or meat display cases. I'd never thought of them as beautiful or warm. I remembered reading once that nomads use horse dung as fuel. I asked Jina if her family did the same. She laughed.

When the snow stopped, we moved again. Every time the box van stopped and I rolled up the door to look outside, the road stretched endlessly, the plains colourless. Because I saw the same landscape each time, it felt like we hadn't moved at all. I couldn't find the sun even looking up at the sky, making it difficult to sense direction. When I held Jina's hand, our bodies resting against each other inside the cargo hold adorned with yellow fairy lights – when I concentrated on the sound of her breathing and the small vibrations through my body – my sense of reality vanished, my past erased. Only the moment existed.

I asked Jina where we were ultimately headed.

—I don't know. One moment they say Finland, the next

Turkey, sometimes Moscow. It keeps changing. They say we have to keep moving anyway.

Which meant no set destination. As much as he tried not to let it show, Jina's father seemed to hesitate at every turn whether to continue west in search of a city or to drive north towards Siberia. The farther west we went, the more likely we were to run into bandits and the virus. The farther north, the worse the cold.

—No. It doesn't matter how far we go. The whole world's like this.

—The whole world?

—Yeah. I see it every night in my dreams.

I looked intently into Jina's ash-coloured eyes. Did she have prophetic dreams?

—It's a joke, silly. You never believe me when I'm serious, but you take all my jokes seriously.

I thought Jina, of all people, might well have prophetic dreams.

—You're looking at me so earnestly I can't even crack a joke.

She cupped my cheeks in her hands, pretending to coddle me.

—Here's what I think. They said there isn't a continent the virus hasn't reached. That was the last news report I heard. There may really be a bunker somewhere, like people say, and I'm sure *someone's* inside. If there are bunkers in Europe, there must be some in Russia. Which means Korea definitely has some too. So why did we come all the way here? How are we going to get into a bunker in Europe when we couldn't find one in Korea? To fire guns with our lives on the line just to reach such a place . . . Dad's probably keeping us on the move because things are volatile and dangerous right now. He needs hope to keep going, so he believes there must be a refugee shelter beyond the border.

Why *did* I leave Korea? Everyone I loved had died. People who used to share the same thoughts and lead similar lives had turned on each other . . . Joy's liver was worth more than a handful of diamonds. I had to keep her safe. Too many people, too many corpses. I couldn't bear it. It was more horrific to suffer in a familiar hell. I was seized by the idea of fleeing to a place I could reach on foot without planes or ships.

—I won't chase after some rumoured bunker. Or put things off any longer.

I repeated Jina's words silently.

—I'd like to start here and now.

Start here and now . . . Start what?

—A new life.

A new . . . How?

As I asked myself these questions, an answer seemed to emerge faintly from the fog of my mind. Like blowing away dust to uncover a forgotten pattern. I was amazed. My first good idea in a while. A resolution as far-fetched as it was good.

*

At the entrance of another ruined village, we encountered a gang of vagabonds, emaciated and starved like zombies. Jina's father shot two dead. The others slowly backed away, glaring at us. Their eyes were wide open, as if determined to remember every one of us inside the box van. My heart had been briefly lit by Jina's wish to start here and now, but a shadow fell over me again. A dark state of mind both comfortable and familiar.

People were outnumbered by revolvers and shotguns. Only men, except Geonji, could carry weapons. Only men could drive or ride in front. Jina's father kept strict tabs on the supplies. We needed his permission to open even a tin of food. The binoculars, the maps, everything was with him. He never slept in the cargo hold with the rest of the family, taking the driver's seat instead with a gun on his chest. He seemed to know that Jina was sleeping outside with me. I didn't know if he warned her when I wasn't around, but he never said anything to me. Still, I remembered what he'd said to me the day we boarded the box van – that I'd have to pay somehow.

Jina wore the lipstick every day. She was always by my side. We slept together, ate together, scavenged through cities together. What I used to never even glance at, what was completely useless in these times, what was easy to procure because it was useless – things like makeup, a hairpin, a scarf, which made Jina happier than anything – became as important as tinned food and matches. I never walked past those things anymore.

I started thinking about whether something would look good on Jina or if she would like it. Geonji, who used to only care about combing his hair in the wing mirror whenever the box van stopped, gradually became one of us. Every time we went scavenging or cooked a tin of food over a fire, Geonji would delight in it like a kid at summer camp. Joy looked up to Geonji. She was sometimes shy, sometimes jealous, sometimes sulky. Perhaps she'd fallen in love.

Jina set her own cutlery, washed it with snow from the plains, dried it clean after every meal. She shook out and folded the blankets daily, always combed her hair before putting on her woolly hat. She never shovelled or poured food in her mouth, never ate straight from the can. She plated it neatly, sat properly, chewed and swallowed slowly. She heated and cooled her food before eating. She put beans in a bowl and ate them one by one as if to confirm, *Ah, this must be a bean*. Even as she bit into a single roasted potato with her back to the wind, Jina's meals reminded me of a leisurely weekend supper. She was born with such nonchalance – a peculiar nonchalance. The ability to retain her dignity even in the depths of hell. She may have been more distressed now for that reason; if she couldn't keep these routines, she'd rather die a hundred times over. As for me, I rushed. I hid in corners so no one would see me eat. If I couldn't heat something up, I ate it cold. To eat as quickly as possible without leaving a trace. To momentarily erase hunger. That was my only reason for eating.

Jina had found another reason.

—I might have to live like this for the rest of my life. This might be my last meal, I don't know. So I want to enjoy it properly, even if it's just a potato. If every day is precious, and every meal is precious, I want to treat precious things preciously.

That might have been Jina's hope. Hope beyond crossing borders or finding bunkers. To live well in the present instead of dwelling on the past or forcing hope on herself.

—Misfortune wants me to mistreat myself. To look down on myself and destroy myself. I'll never let myself resemble this disaster. I won't live as the disaster wants me to live.

I wanted to resemble Jina.

I tried to eat, drink and walk like her. I tried not to rush, to see and feel and think slowly about what was before me. But I wasn't Jina. Jina was unique. We were different. Though I could mimic how she plated her beans before eating them, I could not copy her mind. I was gradually coming to resemble the disaster. I feared Jina would notice.

I had to assume everything had taken a turn for the worse. The absolute worst? A world without Joy. But that hadn't happened. The greatest misfortune stayed one step away, and all I could do was keep constant watch. Sometimes I'd think, *Why do I keep watching?* Like chanting a spell to summon disaster, like I was trying to acclimatise myself. But it was too near, despite my attempts not to look. Every day brought corpses and ruins. What frightened me as much as becoming part of this hellscape was the certainty that I might survive it – condemned to witness such things for the rest of my life. I feared growing indifferent. I feared staying raw. Though surviving each day was technically miraculous, I didn't believe in miracles. There were no miracles anywhere. If they existed, they'd already missed their window. Too many people had died. Say a few survive in the end – would they call that a miracle?

But Jina kept . . . doing things. She made me think differently. She showed me that I could laugh and be happy, even in a situation like this. If someone gave me a tube of lipstick, could I react as happily as Jina did? If not lipstick, what could make me that happy? I couldn't think of anything. Even if my parents were to come back to life right this minute, I wouldn't be able to smile. Or cry. Even if they held my hands and called my name, I'd deny it all, calling it an illusion. Why wouldn't it be? What I found precious, what I loved, what I had to protect, what I missed – I feared all of it. Having Joy was enough. Yet I always looked for Jina. When our eyes met, I'd look away. Even as I secretly imitated her way of speaking and remembered her laugh in the dead of night, I insisted I couldn't get close to her. Like a painkiller, she made me forget reality. I sometimes forgot about Joy when I was with Jina. I let go of Joy's hand several times, only turning around afterwards. Whenever that happened, I resented Jina for no good reason. I resented myself for resenting her. Resentment!

On the road, there's no place for it. You only need to hate or fear. That's how I was before I developed another emotion. Jina gazed at me with such clear eyes when I called her name. Whenever I saw her eyes, I wondered about mine. *How do I look at you? What kind of look could it be that makes you see me and smile?*

—Jina.

Jina turned to me. I held out a card I'd picked up in the last village. A small card with a red Christmas tree illustration. Inside was a short message in Russian I couldn't decipher. When I spotted that card in a scattered pile of rubbish, I'd been shaken. I felt nauseated, like I was carsick. I recalled the greetings I used to exchange during the festive seasons . . . All those sleepless nights spent flipping through diary pages I'd filled that year. One year, I wandered around a stationery shop to buy myself a new diary. Surrounded by fairy lights and carols. Hearing countless calls of *Merry Christmas!* and *Happy New Year!* as I walked down the street alone. I rolled those phrases around in my mouth. What was the date today? Had the new year already begun? There was no longer any meaning in such things. We were walking in the heart of winter. Here, no one aged and time didn't pass in days and years. I wouldn't be surprised if spring arrived and slid straight into summer, if I looked at a clear lake and saw an old woman in my reflection. Looking at the Russian handwriting on the card, I recalled the Merry Christmases and Happy New

Years I now had to forget. Jina wouldn't be like this. She'd spend precious days preciously.

Jina laughed as only Jina could and accepted the card.

I'd like to laugh like Jina, I thought, when I found myself kissing her. It was cold and warm. Rough and soft. Frostbite and hunger and misfortune and disaster all bolted away, surprised by our kiss.

My lips, too, smelled of roses.

We followed the river to a small village. Like all the others we'd seen, every vegetable garden had a small house attached like a growth. There were vacant houses and houses with people inside. The villagers wore clean clothes. They looked healthy. They kept an appropriate distance from us but didn't try to drive us out. They seemed to wish we'd quietly pass through. We decided to park the box vans in the vegetable garden at the edge of the village and rest for a night. Water trickled out when we turned the tap. Jina said she was happy to sleep in a place worthy of being called a house for the first time in ages. The others didn't want to sleep indoors. They kept their guards up, saying the villagers could turn at any moment and rob us. The men did not let go of their guns, even as they started a fire and heated food.

As soon as we stepped into the house, Jina held her rucksack upside down and shook its contents out. All sorts of junk poured out like scampering children. The things that Jina brought from Korea and the things we scavenged from the road were all tangled together, forming a modest mound. I was startled to see a thin book alongside a pair of earphones. They felt like inventions from the future. I couldn't believe she'd thought to pack a book and earphones in an emergency.

Seeing those earphones, I wanted to listen to music.

Seeing that ballpoint pen, I wanted to write. I wanted to scribble, to write letters.

Seeing that book, I wanted to read sentences. I wanted to dissolve the sentences one by one in my mouth and swallow them. Touching the smooth cover and gazing at the title, *Annam*, for a long time, I opened the thin book to a random page. I held it up to the fire.

They died alone, far from their country, and far from war.

I put the book down.

The sentence wounded me. One by one, the words rolled down and crashed like boulders before my eyes. I couldn't process the line despite its brevity.

—Want to read it? I really like that book.

I felt even more inclined to read it since Jina liked it, but considering how much a single sentence could shock me . . . I didn't think I could read the whole thing. I slowly shook my head.

—Try it. I'll give it to you as a present. A Christmas present. You gave me one.

With a playful chuckle, Jina placed the book inside my overcoat. I adjusted my coat as I recalled the sentence I'd just read. The words turned into sharp rocks rolling painfully inside my head.

Geonji mumbled,

—But today's not Christmas.

—Everyone has a Christmas of their own. If you don't have one, you should make one too.

Jina suddenly grabbed a plastic pouch from the pile she was digging through. It was a travel toiletry set, an object as astounding as the earphones had been. She made an announcement.

—Let's take a bath.

Jina held out a disposable razor to Geonji.

—You should shave a little. I can give you a haircut too if you want.

Running his fingers through his hair, Geonji feigned disgust.

—Don't I kind of look like Won Bin with my hair grown out?

I was surprised again. *Won Bin*. What an incredible thing to say. A name I hadn't thought of even once since the disaster. Geonji made a habit of combing his hair in the side mirror. Had he been thinking about an actor all along?

—Or maybe Kang Dong-won, depending on the day.

Geonji kept saying these incredible things. Jina didn't even pretend to listen. Joy stared only at his lips. Inside this decent house – sitting between Jina and Geonji, who held their heads high even when met with misfortune and despair – I goofed around for the first time in ages. I poked fun at Geonji and shared childhood stories. I laughed, and it wasn't a dream.

I lit a candle and put a glass cover over it, lighting up the bathroom. Jina, Joy and I filled the bathtub with water we'd boiled outside, then undressed side by side. Bodies so scrawny that our bones looked ready to pierce the skin any minute. Moving cast a shadow between each and every bone. Jina and I bathed Joy first with the warm water and a single bar of soap.

Jina muttered, wiping Joy's back.

—You're so thin, I don't know where to touch.

We were all like that. How nice it would be if we didn't die from getting thinner, but simply grew small like dust. Then no one would be able to hurt us. Jina looked at me and commented on my skin. My body was pale, but my face and hands were the colour of earth. I wanted to look at my whole body, but I could only see down to my collarbones in the bathroom mirror. My reflection, which I hadn't seen in a while, felt unfamiliar and awkward. But splashing myself with warm water and simply being close to Jina made me feel free. We shared silly jokes and kept giggling as if under a spell. Joy watched me uneasily as I laughed.

I tapped my chin with my right little finger.

—It's fine.

I dried Joy's wet body.

—It's because you're pretty.

Jina tapped her chin with her little finger.

—Does this mean 'fine'?

—Yeah.

—How about this?

—'Pretty.'

—Ah.

Jina put her index finger on Joy's dimple and rotated it slightly. I dressed Joy in her long johns and let her out first; only the two of us remained. Jina's hair looked even redder when wet. White steam bloomed from our bodies soaked in warm water. I pulled her towards me and we stood in front of the mirror together. I was more used to Jina's face than my own. I could look at her with ease. Gazing at her reflection, I stroked her hair. She was warm. Her earlobes were soft, and the curve of her neck was like that of a violin. I traced my fingers against her skin as if stroking violin strings, before slightly rotating my index finger on her cheek. Suddenly I remembered Dad's last moments. I remembered the people who'd died. I remembered the man whose neck I'd sliced open with my jackknife. I was reminded of the gushing blood – of the night I spent in the forest, covered in that blood, erasing the memory in blood-stiffened clothes and with cold eyes. All at once, I remembered the blows that had fallen like hail and the languages I couldn't understand. I almost considered myself lucky. To be alive like this. Had the world remained as before, could I have met Jina? Noticing my frozen expression,

Jina hugged me tightly. She patted me gently on the back and stroked my head. She tapped my chin twice with her little finger. That gesture, meaning *fine*, became her knock at my door, and we kissed as though we were magnetically drawn to each other. All the spite inside my body melted away. Jina led me to the bathtub. In the warm water, I leaned against Jina and found her lips again and again. I found her soft breasts, the bridge of her nose, her eyelashes.

—We're starting here and now.

I remembered Jina's words that had been hidden in the shade. *You only live once, and there's no such thing as 'what if'. The world is coming to an end, but we found each other. That makes it fine. We could even consider ourselves lucky in this moment.*

Geonji urgently knocked on the door.

—Hey, when are you getting out? I want to have a wash too.

I want to live each day as though it were a lifetime. I want to become Jina. If I can't, I'd rather leave her side. I want to stop feeling the differences between us. Fearing separation, we embraced to become one, as if to show each other our bare hearts, as if to check what *this* was before naming it. As if sharing each other in this way was our only hope brushing past us.

Geonji

Fresh from my bath, feeling clean for once, I stepped outside with Joy. Some of the family had a fire going and gave me a bit of reheated lamb. I grabbed my sleeping bag from the box van and headed back towards Jina and Dori. That's when gunmen came out of the dark. Jina's dad tried to negotiate, but they wanted everything: food, fuel, the box vans, even the women. When he moved to run them down, they scattered, opening fire. I pulled Joy tight and shoved us into the shadows, back against a wall. Gunshots cracked through the night. I couldn't tell where the bullets were coming from, or where they were landing. Chaos. Joy was screaming, choking on her own sobs.

—Don't worry, Joy. Dori's in the house. She'll be fine. Just make sure you're safe.

I whispered to calm her down, but there was no way she heard me. I had no choice: my hand clamped over her mouth. My palm practically swallowed her, it was so big, her face so tiny. I was terrified. I wanted to burrow into the earth like a mole. Just then, Dori ran out of the house. She looked around for Joy without even crouching, like the bullets meant nothing to her. Jina started to follow, but Dori shoved her back as bullet casings pinged off the door and window frames. One of the box vans whipped around the vegetable garden and braked hard, blocking the front door. The gunfire got heavier. I yelled for Dori. She grabbed Joy and ran back inside, then dropped to her stomach. She was crying.

When the shooting stopped, I glanced outside. Some people were running towards the main road. The gunshots started again. Two runners stumbled. One fell while the other limped on. Jina's dad climbed out of the box van and checked the bodies. He cursed. The family crawled out from their hiding spots and gathered around him. Taewoo was sprawled on the ground. Jina's dad grabbed her chin, forcing her to look at Taewoo.

—Take a good look at who died.

He spat out the words like old gum.

—This could've been you.

Jina closed her eyes. He shoved her into the box van like an animal, then turned on Dori.

—My daughter almost died because of you!

—But she didn't.

—She would have if it weren't for me!

—And I could die because of her too.

Jina's dad slapped Dori. I froze. He'd never hit anyone who wasn't trying to rob us. Never even really yelled. But he hit

Dori. Jina jumped from the box van. Even as she stumbled, Dori pulled Joy's knit hat down to her chin and passed her to me.

—If I had a gun, I would've fired it. Just like you.

He hit her again. Jina tried to hold him back, clinging to him in tears.

—Stop it, Dad. I probably could've saved him.

—Oh, you think I should just hand over my gun to you?

Every blow sent Dori staggering back. Jina screamed, clutching at her dad, but he didn't budge. He just threw her off like a giant tree in a hurricane and kept beating Dori. The other adults watched, their eyes glinting in the dark. In their minds, Dori had killed Taewoo, nearly killed Jina, and would keep bringing death wherever she went. None of this would've happened without her.

A tyre had blown out, and there were bullet holes all over the cargo hold. The adults scrambled to patch the damage and set up guard shifts. Dori slipped into the empty house with Joy while Jina's dad locked Jina in the box van. The older guys took watch, passing a bottle of vodka around. I frantically searched the vegetable garden and nearby bushes for dry branches, terrified the fire would die. The bandits could come back the second it went out. The sky was dark and moonless. I couldn't get Dori's battered face out of my head – her lips all split open and bloody, maybe some teeth broken. The guilt was eating me alive. I'd just stood there like a coward when he hit her. Didn't even try to stop him. I hated myself for it. Exactly like school all over again. I thought about boiling water for Dori. She'd need it to clean her wounds. Plus, she liked warm things. She liked holding a cup of warm water with both hands and sipping it slowly. Why did Jina's dad beat Dori? Why was he blaming everything on her? I was still in shock about Taewoo. I couldn't believe he was actually dead. We weren't close. He treated me like a kid and talked rough, but he'd offered to teach me how to drive once and gave me a shot of vodka when the adults weren't looking. 'A man should know how to throw back a drink,' he'd said, teaching me how to hold my breath.

Auntie sat there holding Taewoo's body, crying without making a sound.

—My beautiful boy . . . my son, so young, who never got to marry. He survived everything just to get shot in some foreign country.

She stared up at the night sky.

—If you had to take someone, why not those useless bitches? Why did it have to be my precious son?

Her words freaked me out. Kids at school used to call me a shitstain. Whenever they got yelled at by teachers, or got dumped by their girlfriends, or didn't get their allowance, or got bullied by older kids – whenever they dropped their food, or it was rainy or windy, or flies were buzzing, or they were pissed off for any reason, they blamed it on me. They beat me up because of it. They never had trouble finding an excuse to hit me. The world existed to prove that I was, in fact, a shitstain. My old man did it too. He said everything was my fault and Mum's fault. That we were ruining his life. But it was actually the other way around. He ruined our family. After Mum died and he had no one left to blame, he killed himself.

Dori wouldn't be able to leave with us, no matter how much Jina begged.

I really wanted Dori to know I wasn't like the others, even though I'd failed to stop Jina's dad. Would that even make a difference to her? But Dori wasn't someone who needed comfort. She just ran from that kind of thing. Still, as I heated the water, I wondered if something like this would help. If I didn't at least bring her warm water – if I didn't walk over with some excuse – I'd probably never see her again.

Avoiding the adults, I slipped in through the back door and swept my torch across the dark living room. There, in a sleeping bag, was Joy, frowning even while asleep. I set the warm water down and called softly for Dori. Then I heard it: dull thuds from deeper in the house. The bathroom, maybe. I called Dori's name again, louder. Swearing came from behind a door. I froze. Moaning. Muffled sounds. Scuffling. The sounds of a struggle. Someone being pushed around. I ran to the bathroom door. It was locked. I kicked it until the wood splintered, reached through and turned the lock. Dori had been shoved into the tub, gagged and shaking. Her trousers were gone. She clutched the jackknife in trembling hands, blood matting her hair and streaking her face. But her eyes burned right through me. Eyes that didn't shrink from the light but shot it right back. I couldn't move. I was trapped in that stare.

An instant. Thirty, ten, no – it couldn't have been more than five seconds. But it felt like forever. I was scared. It was intense. Everything felt so slow, like my heart had stopped, but I was out of breath, and all the years I'd lived poured out in that breathless moment. I felt every feeling I'd ever had. I searched for something familiar. Did I know anything close to this?

Dori cut the gag with her jackknife. She slipped trying to get up from the tub. I walked over and helped her out. Little Uncle was sprawled on the bathroom floor, blood gushing from his neck. Dori pulled her clothes back on and picked a revolver up off the floor. It was the one Little Uncle always carried. Dori stumbled out to the living room, hugged Joy and gently shook her awake.

—The water, over there . . .

Our eyes met. I couldn't see very well in the dark, but I definitely felt it.

—It should be warm. Wash your face.

Her eyes stayed on mine as she shoved the sleeping bag into her pack.

—Hurry. Joy's going to freak if she sees.

—Why did you come.

Her voice was barely a whisper.

—Were you going to . . . like that bastard . . .

—No! Seriously, Jina? You think I'm crazy?

—Then why.

—Because I'm worried. You know why.

I got closer and helped her pack up. She scooped some water and rinsed the blood off her face. Just then, I heard the front door open.

—Still at it?

It was Big Uncle. He'd been drinking vodka during his guard shift.

—Just finish up already. Seongcheol's waiting, too.

Dori woke Joy, stepped in front of her and threw on her rucksack.

—What about the mute? What are we doing with her?

That was Seongcheol.

—We have to make good money off her. Those crazy bastards out to eat kid liver . . .

Big Uncle kept ranting, turning the doorknob. Dori and I held our breath, waiting for the door to shut. Then he just stopped mid-sentence. Dori slowly raised the revolver to her chest. Silence and darkness choked the house. Suddenly, a beam of torchlight poured into the living room.

—Wait a minute.

I said it first. Big Uncle realised what was happening and quickly pulled out his gun. Dori aimed back at him. If anyone shot, it was over. I got between them, trying to block their view. Big Uncle yelled for backup. It was obvious. They were going to kill Dori. *What now? What do I do?* I looked around. There was a window behind Dori. And a road past that window.

—Window.

I whispered, then tackled Big Uncle. I heard a gunshot. We wrestled. All the adults ran inside. Beams of torchlight cluttered the living room. Someone saw the bathroom and cursed. They cursed and damned Dori. They damned her and cried.

—We have to catch that fucking bitch right now and kill her.

Big Uncle kicked me, slammed me into a corner and stomped on me. They'd tried to rape her. At least three of them. Maybe Jina's dad too. How many times had this happened? Had Dori ever been safe? I'd thought she'd be safe with us, thought the adults were protecting us with their guns and box vans. I'd believed horrible, dangerous people only existed outside our convoy. How far would Dori go now? Would I ever see her again? I should've stopped Jina's dad when he hit her. Should've never left her alone. If I had stayed, maybe none of this would've happened. Or maybe it always would have.

When her eyes locked on mine, I felt something. I know the word. But I won't say it. I'll keep it a secret until I die. And I won't forget. If this happens again – if someone tries to beat or kill me – I'll remember the way Dori looked at me. I'll never forgive.

Jina

If I let daybreak come like this, Dori would disappear forever. I had to find a way to be with her. I slipped out of the box van without alerting my father, but couldn't run straight to the house. The older folks were in the vegetable garden. I was circling to the back door when I heard Big Uncle calling people over from inside the house. Why was he inside? I raced to the door. With the sound of gunfire, a small shadow burst out of a window. Two tangled shadows darted down the dark road. I called out to her exactly once, but Dori only glanced back. She kept running, and I ran after her. I heard gunfire coming from the window. It was the older folks. I turned and screamed for them to stop. The shooting stopped. They called my name to check on me. I looked around for Dori, but she'd already vanished. Even when I ran and ran in the direction she'd disappeared, I only found a deep darkness. The trees wailed with the wind. With each cry the darkness grew deeper, my body heavier. I couldn't keep my balance as I tried to stand still and breathe. I stumbled a few steps before dropping to the ground. I felt trapped in the dark.

—Jina.

I looked around. Dark houses. Dark windows. Trees bristling with dark thorns. Snow swirling in the wind.

—I have to go.

I spun around, panting. I could only hear her voice.

—I killed your uncle.

I froze.

—I'm not sure. He's probably dead.

I couldn't speak.

—He raped me.

Her voice cracked.

—Jina.

Dori called my name like it was a question.

—Do you want to come with me?

Everything stopped. I looked back at the bouncing beams of torchlight in the distance. I couldn't answer. I couldn't decide. I couldn't let them go . . . but let go of whom? The beams bounced closer. They were running to kill Dori. On the road, hesitation only brought suffering.

I shook my head.

Feet pounded towards us. Two small, dark shadows disappeared between the giant pine trees. Tears flooded my eyes. *Where are you going? Where?* Multiple footsteps pounded closer, then ran past me. *Where am I supposed to go?* A thick hand caught my shoulder. I shuddered as if he'd doused me in sewage. I screamed at him to get off me. Everyone was bad. Everyone who didn't die, who survived, who couldn't help but keep living like this, was bad. If we survived, if we somehow survived these horrors, we shouldn't be this way. It was possible for us *not* to be this way. Why were we destroying everything? Why were we making everything worse?

Snow fell down.

Daybreak came slowly.

I trimmed Dori's nails with rusty scissors from the kitchen. Her nails cracked like dried bark at the metal's slightest touch. I held the torch over the clippings.

—Does it hurt?

Dori shook her head, speaking slowly and softly.

—A little, but it's okay. I like when you touch them.

I pressed my tongue to her fingertips, wetting them with saliva as I finished clipping.

—I'll cut your hair when the sun comes up. Give you a cute bob.

Wind rattled the window. Our shadows danced slowly on the wall in the candlelight.

—Do you know this song?

Dori hummed quietly. I'd never heard it.

—What's it called?

—'Ma rendi pur contento', I think.

—Ma rendi pur . . .

—Contento.

—What does that mean?

Dori shook her head. She'd first heard it last spring on a late-night radio show.

—I loved it so much I wrote down the title and played it constantly. I kept meaning to look up the lyrics, but never did. Should've done it while we still had internet. Now I'll never know.

—Where's it from?

—Italian opera. I don't even know what it's about, but it haunts me. I must've hummed it to myself thousands of times walking with Joy.

—Do you still do that?

Dori nodded. I'd always wondered what she was thinking whenever she stared off with that distant look. She was repeating this unknowable song. I tried to imagine Dori's mind – recalling Italian opera on Russian soil, thinking, *Now I'll never know what it means.*

—Dori, that's exactly how I see you.

—What?

—I keep thinking about you without knowing what's inside.

Dori laughed a little and studied my face.

—Weren't you surprised when you first saw me?

—When I first saw you?

—Yeah.

—Of course.

—You didn't act like it. Just came over and started talking to me.

—I was in awe. That's why.

—In awe?

—Yeah. You were like a mirage. Like someone had placed you there. I needed to make sure you were real. But you didn't answer. Didn't even smile.

—I was scared.

—When you first saw me?

—Yeah.

—Why?

—Because you're human.

—. . . When we were little, we only had to fear ghosts.

—You'd still scream if you saw one now.

—My mum used to see ghosts.

—Did she talk to them?

—No. She said they'd disappear once she recognised what they were.

—Maybe ghosts are scared of humans too.

—I had a friend at school who could really sing. Super shy, barely talked and went red just standing in front of people . . . But when she sang, she became someone else. Made me realise what it meant to be born with talent. I kept thinking I'd hear about her after we finished school, that she'd become a singer. Then . . . walking home from work one night, a stranger . . . You know how they call some murders random?

—. . .

—People say it's random. Like there's no reason. Someone dies and they say there's no reason. I didn't understand then, but now I'm too scared to know the reason. Ghosts don't frighten me anymore.

—Jina.

Dori pulled out her jackknife and held it out to me.

—Do you want this?

— . . . Why?

— . . .

—This is yours now. Don't lose it, don't give it away, don't let anyone take it. With every new person you meet, act like you did when you first met me.

—Someone could die from a tiny thing like this.

—Exactly.

— . . .

—Don't die, Dori.

— . . .

—Whatever happens, we have to survive together.

—Together? How?

—We can if we stay together.

We were still talking, still gazing at each other when gunshots rang out. Dori ran to find Joy. She cried. She was beaten and trapped. I'd promised we'd stay together. I'd brought it up. That wasn't even a day ago.

How could she kill someone over something like that? She's vicious, depraved, they murmured. *She's probably killed others. Must've been robbing people in Korea before coming here.*

No wonder she never talked about herself. We brought a murderer all the way out here. If she'd cooperated, we could've let her go peacefully with her sister. In this world we live in, it's not that big a deal to let someone have a go at your body. I mean, did she think she'd ride for free?

—They've all lost their minds.

—Your uncle is dead.

—Dad, did you know about this?

—That bitch killed my brother.

—Were you in on it too?

—Two family members are dead because of that bitch!

—I'll end up like that someday, won't I?

—That's never happening. You think I'd let that happen?

—You don't think they'll touch me? Because I'm family?

—Don't insult your family.

—I didn't insult them. They insulted themselves.

—Jina. Snap out of it.

I shook my head.

—I don't know. There's no such thing as 'never happening'.

His face went rigid.

—She mocked us. We treated her like family, but she was using us. Never showed respect, even after putting you in danger. She's rotten.

My father was lying.

—You're not a good judge of character yet. You think everyone's good as long as you like them.

I wanted to spit in his face. I felt sorry for him. I was terrified of him. He loved me and I loved him, but I wanted to spit at him. If he had raped and killed Dori – no, how was that possible? But it could've happened.

—I never suspected family. There's no good or bad when it comes to family. You know how many times I told her our family would never do anything wrong? But we're all plenty wrong. We're capable of worse. I know that now. So I'll protect myself. You protect yourself. Please, protect yourself from becoming worse!

Father grabbed my shoulders and shook me.

—Look closely at who's going to protect you!

I looked around. My relatives watched me, completely destroyed, sobbing. I remembered their names. Not Uncle or Auntie, but their actual names. Matching names to faces, these people became strangers. I didn't see family. We could easily betray each other. Beat and abandon each other. Rape and kill each other. My father's belief that family would never hurt each other was thin as Bible pages. He'd driven Dori away to protect that fragile thing. I knew my father would do anything for me. Was that why he tried to beat, rape and kill Dori? Who was that actually for? These terrible questions.

The family agreed they couldn't forgive Geonji. *Would he have helped Dori if it'd been his own uncle bleeding on the floor? This is why you don't take in strays.* But I couldn't send Geonji away too. I'd lose my mirror. Like a honeybee among wasps,

I'd think I was a wasp and eventually become one. I'd live as a wasp. I'd mock flowers and honey and butterflies. I clung to Geonji and cried. I begged him not to leave.

—It's fine, Jina. Don't cry. Don't worry. We'll meet again.

That's what he said.

Ryu

As I pulled away, leaving the sisters on the road with just a few cans, I watched them grow smaller in the wing mirror. The realisation crept in: I was abandoning something precious. The little one looked around Haerim's age. The older girl watched me with cold, guarded eyes. She seemed to accept my gesture as nothing more than a transaction. Would those girls survive? How far would they get? My worry twisted into alarm. Would *we* survive? How far would *we* get? I tried to stop thinking. I wanted never to see them on the road again, to forget them entirely. But my memories were strangely linked – whenever I thought about Haerim, I was reminded of those two girls. And I always thought about Haerim.

Dan wanted to cross the border into Europe. He believed that a system for survivors would be in place there, that we could start fresh. To me, this sounded no different from a sermon promising heaven.

There was a time when we looked everything up on our phones, when we lived according to information received through virtual windows, worshipping the latest technologies like gods. Dan hadn't moved on from those days. He tried to solve present problems with past logic, longing for a new life that was identical to the world we had already lived in and lost. News outlets and social media overflowed with information after the virus struck, just as they had before. The live updates refreshed too quickly. I couldn't distinguish real from fake. Certain information, inflated by rumour and conspiracy, prevailed and turned the real disaster into a joke. So we grew numb. Concern cooled to indifference, and we shrugged it all off. *Oh, this again. I'm sure it'll be fine eventually.* But now we didn't need the news to know the truth. We saw the ruins and corpses, the bandits and looters on the road. That was our world. We had all become refugees.

Some people resist waking, pushing morning away the harder you try to rouse them from sleep. My only wish was for Dan not to lose his mind.

That said, I wanted to believe in Dan, who was certain that a new world would appear once we crossed this vast continent and its borders. If there was a world where I could still dream of tomorrow without needing miracles, I wanted to make a grave for Haerim there. I wanted to burn her pyjamas from Korea, bury the ashes in safe ground, and plant a tree as a small marker. I wanted to watch that tree grow little by little.

We drove for over two weeks. We slept in the car and ate in the car. Our limbs grew stiff and our headaches never let up.

We tried to fill the tank in every city we passed through, but it wasn't easy. Driving down that endless road, I couldn't stop thinking about where we were headed, and why. It felt like running on a hamster wheel. *Isn't there another way besides charging forward like this? What if we're the only ones who haven't figured it out? There's no way everyone else is wasting their time like this*... These thoughts weren't new. The same doubts that had followed me into adulthood, questions I'd been asking myself long before the virus shrouded the world... How was it that I had the same thoughts, even after everything we'd been through to escape Korea? I was ultimately no different from Dan – the global catastrophe had changed neither my thought process nor my concerns. I was like an outdated GPS system. Or someone who would ask the same question in any situation. Someone who would worry about better options even as they drew their last breath.

We parked on the outskirts of the city. If we couldn't fill our tank here, we had no choice but to abandon the car and continue on foot or wait until we found petrol. The city was bleak and deserted. With each gust of winter wind, hollow laughter echoed through the buildings. A deranged man staggered past, shaking his fist at thin air.

Dan got out to look for supplies. Through the rearview mirror, I watched Haemin sleep. I thought he'd wake up any moment and ask when we were going home. My mind reeled whenever he said something like that. What would it have been like if we hadn't left Korea? Could we have kept Haemin safe? No amount of driving could erase my memories of that place. Streets filled with wailing madness, people consumed by rage and fear, killing and breaking and burning whatever was in front of them. Those memories didn't seem to drift away – they actively chased after us. Like a creature charging at us at hurricane speed. Were we really alive? Or had we already died and descended into hell? What if this was our punishment? Forever in fear. Forever on the run.

Dan used to fall asleep on the living room sofa watching TV. I couldn't sleep with any light or sound on. When I closed the bedroom door and lay in bed, I only became more sensitive to the muffled sound of the TV. Many nights, I hung by a thread of sleep, waiting for the alarm to ring. When it did, I'd wake the kids and Dan, prepare toast or soup with rice for them, and see them off. I barely had time to wash my face and throw on whatever clothes were to hand before leaving the house myself.

I handled consultation and clerical work at a downtown travel agency. Bangkok, Phuket, Cebu, Boracay, Hanoi, Taipei, Bali . . . I peddled destinations I knew only by name, crafting itineraries for clients while pretending I'd vacationed there hundreds of times. Back then, the world didn't seem vast at all. I thought the Earth was quite small, considering how clients could reach distant countries in a day or two by plane. I crossed time zones like a frequent flyer in my own way – summer felt like just the day before yesterday, and suddenly it was the holiday season. The months between Chuseok and the Lunar New Year blurred into mere days, and before I knew it, the whole year had flown by. I tracked each month by payday. Money drained from my bank account on set dates. Despite our steady incomes, we were always pinched for cash. We postponed important events or rushed through them cursorily: family vacations, family photos, birthday parties. Even compliments and consolations, greetings like 'How was your day?' or 'You've grown so tall!' were hurried. We'd hardly manage a real hug or say 'I love you', failing to truly cherish today or look forward to tomorrow. We barely watched over each other, barely wished each other good night.

I'd come to my senses only to find myself yelling at the kids. It was no use trying to compose myself, telling myself not to act this way. If not the kids, then I'd erupt at the plates in the kitchen sink. I'd rage at the laundry tangled in the washing machine, or the noisy vacuum cleaner in my hand. Even the dust floating in the air could ignite my fury. I used the kids' lotion because I couldn't make time to buy my own. I wore my autumn windbreaker through the bitter end of the year, catching a nasty cold because there was no time to drop my winter coats off at the dry cleaner. Dead houseplants, expired food, off-season clothes, worn-out shoes, recyclable boxes and broken objects piled up around the house, never finding their place. The house grew smaller, the kids' secrets multiplied, Dan spoke less, and I withered. I was certainly trying my best, but the thought that my best wasn't good enough would catch up with me twice a year or so. Life staggered on, severed at every joint. Me at work, me in front of the kids, me talking to Dan, and me alone – all repulsively different. This person called 'me' felt like a scattered puzzle. I couldn't remember what the original picture was supposed to look like. It felt like something was ever so slightly askew, something that would eventually dislocate everything. Me from myself. Me from Dan. Me from my children.

Once, Haerim hurt herself badly falling down the stairs at after-school tutoring. She had scratches on her face, bruises all over her body and a cast on her arm. After pleading with my boss, I didn't go into work for three days. I went over budget on a single room at the hospital. I watched over Haerim and Haemin in that clean, quiet room. Those days with my children felt like a vacation, like the chocolate plaque on a cake, a 'Congratulations!' written in cursive. Even complaining that her sides hurt, Haerim laughed often and ate the hospital food without a single complaint about the side dishes.

Though Haemin didn't get hurt – or I assumed he hadn't – he carried scars I knew little about. Hyeonsu kept kicking him at school, and their kindergarten teacher merely told them to play nice and get along. There was also an older kid in his taekwondo class who called him a 'fucking prick' and bullied him, so Haemin called him a 'fucking prick' back. Then he was called up to the rooftop stairway and threatened: 'The next time you get on my nerves, I'm going to stab your family to death and burn your house down.' Terrified his mum, dad and older sister would die because of him, Haemin followed the older kid's orders to steal a bottle of soju from the convenience store. Later, kicking a football around by himself in the playground, the ball got stuck in the fence. His clothes got dirty and his hands scratched raw as he tried to retrieve it, worried I'd yell at him if he lost the ball. But then it got stuck even deeper. When he eventually came home empty-handed, I was too busy with life to notice the football had disappeared . . .

—Huh? What was I busy with?

—With life. Mum, you said it yourself.

—When did I say that?

—I dunno. But you said it.

I believed family came first. That I couldn't give up on them. But I had no time to be with them. If I didn't work, we'd be poor, and if we were poor, the kids would get hurt. They already struggled to make friends. If they didn't live in a luxury apartment or attend tutoring like everyone else did, they were bullied. Could parental love alone heal those scars? I didn't know how to brush off dirty looks and disrespect, so I couldn't teach my kids either. Books and certain TV shows offered instructions, but it was like learning to cook with a recipe and no kitchen. It was actually easier to make money. To bring my children's living conditions up to average, I had to sacrifice my time with them.

There was a period when Dan started coming home

ridiculously late – this was right when Haerim had just started school. Two, three in the morning, a couple of times a week. For the first few months, he'd return completely drunk. Then for about half a year, he'd come home sober but still well past midnight. Some nights he didn't come home at all. I suspected he was having an affair, but I chose not to acknowledge it. I didn't have the energy for the inevitable confrontations and tears. I wanted to avoid the inevitable emotional chaos that would follow once he realised I knew. Divorce felt overwhelming, though I'd considered it briefly. Simply managing each day was difficult enough. I decided that if he was going to return to our family, he would – and he did. We resumed our usual routines. Without confessions or explanations, I buried the knowledge as though nothing had happened. I thought perhaps when we were much older, when there was no turning back, I might ask him about it then. I didn't want to carry that pain now.

Am I living well? I can't recall when this question first surfaced. Was it even possible to live well? I believe that's where everything began, with those questions. Before graduating college, I feared the uncertainty ahead but remained optimistic that things would somehow resolve themselves. After moving between several companies for three years, I joined a makeup distribution firm. My role involved bringing American products to Korea – at least it related to my field of study. I was commuting between work and home when I met Dan through a mutual college acquaintance. We would meet for dinner or coffee occasionally. Neither of us could manage frequent meetings or daily phone calls due to our schedules, but we maintained contact every few days. When either of us mentioned being too busy to call, the other accepted it without question. We continued this pattern for nearly a year. Work took precedence over dating or marriage, and our connection was neither passionate enough to call love nor distant enough to end.

When a three-day weekend arrived that summer, Dan suggested a late-night movie. We left the cinema after four in the morning. I had stayed up that late for work obligations before – overtime, company functions – but I hadn't experienced dawn like that in years. Simply because I wanted to, not because I was required to. Dan and I ate instant noodles and kimbap at a convenience store and walked to a small neighbourhood park with ice cream. It was our first real date.

—I only have a bed and a fridge in my apartment.

Dan blurted out.

—Gas cooker, dining table, sofa, desk, TV . . . I don't own any of those things. Because I only sleep there.

I wasn't any different. My room was too small for that kind of furniture anyway.

—Now that I've been living like this for several years, I wonder if this is really the life I wanted. Every morning during my commute, I tell myself this is sufficient, but by the evening when I'm heading home, I can't stop questioning it.

The same thought visited me daily. The sensation of sitting

alone on a playground swing, moving back and forth between *This is fine* and *Is this fine*?

—If I ever get married, I'll start living properly. Officially. For real.

I chuckled. What he said took me back to my senior year of high school, when I promised myself I'd lose weight and start dating and live like a real person once I got to college. And then my senior year in college, when I swore I'd go see plays and take weekend trips and see friends constantly and learn violin as soon as I had a stable job. I felt a wave of relief knowing that Dan and I were fundamentally the same kind of person. It was precisely what I'd been looking for in a partner – not excitement or passion, but that sense of recognition. Our relationship began this way and continued without significant conflicts or reconciliations. We weren't mistrustful or possessive; we didn't meddle in each other's lives or criticise. Did we ever say 'I love you'? I'm not certain. There were moments when those words seemed necessary, but they always passed without being spoken. 'We should see a musical sometime.' 'Let's make sure we visit that art exhibition next month.' 'We really need to take that weekend trip to Jeju Island this year.' I think we confirmed our feelings through these empty promises we made to each other. Marriage was the only promise we actually kept among all the ones we made. Then Haerim was born. Since no one told me they loved me, I never passed those words along to her. But the year she turned five, Haerim said, 'I love you, Mum.' When I hugged my sweet little child, she . . .

I startled awake. Dan was knocking on the car window, gesturing for me to unlock the door. I fumbled with the lock and let him in. He immediately crouched low and aimed his gun towards the windshield. A dark mass was moving slowly towards us in the distance. It looked like an enormous beast with black fur. The tender sensation of Haerim embracing me still lingered in my stiff body. Had that been a dream? I had lived through that moment, but somehow reality had transformed into a dream. I glanced at Haemin. I wasn't sure when he'd awakened, but he was staring straight ahead, his eyes wide.

—Hide under your seat.

Haemin obeyed without crying or protesting. The dark mass continued to grow larger as it approached. It felt like our fate, our inner selves, the shadow of our anxieties and fears all lumped together. I realised I wouldn't be shocked by whatever this turned out to be. I no longer had the capacity for shock.

—They're people. I count at least two or three hundred of them.

Dan was trembling, even as he kept his gun trained ahead. If this many people intended to attack us, the logical thing would be for Dan to shoot Haemin and me first, then himself.

A sound reached us before the people did, low and rough like smoke. They were singing, their voices flowing in murmured melodies, holding crosses and white flags like mourners in a funeral procession. They stumbled, worn and sorrowful. Sobbing as if pleading, they passed by us as calmly as a river. I got out of the car, transfixed. Dan held me back. I wanted to ask them: Where did you come from? Where are you going? What are you singing? They were all singing different songs. The melodies layered over each other, reaching us as one enormous sound. I moved into the crowd. I needed to find someone I could speak with. I pieced together conversation using English and Korean. A bony woman seized my wrist. I could barely make out what she was saying through her sobs. She told me there were armed gangs at every border, killing people and taking their belongings. They were growing their ranks. Cities had become human slaughterhouses. Those who survived, breathing in the smoke and stench from burning bodies, were losing their minds. War continued without pause, day and night. A red stream flowed across the frozen ground, and everything had been destroyed. The woman held onto me tightly.

—We have to stay together. We can't let them kill us. This world is hell now. We're already damned just for being alive. But we have to hold on to each other. We have to look at each other, touch each other, sing together. Otherwise we'll forget what it means to be human.

I lifted my head and looked around. There were faces in windows - not many, but some people emerged from buildings and joined the procession.

Dan grabbed my hand and pulled me back from the crowd. I told him what the woman had said. He shook his head.

—We can't believe everything crazy people tell us.

—Maybe she's crazy. But there were children with them. That means they haven't lost their minds enough to sell children or eat their livers.

Dan bit his lips, his expression torn. *Let's follow them.* I barely managed to swallow those words rising in my throat. He was struggling with something too. He chewed his lip and exhaled sharply. We stood there on the road, postponing any decision, until we could no longer separate the singing from the sound of wind. Were their words truth or prophecy? Should we head for the border or remain here? The closest border was Kazakhstan. Were there gangs there as well? What would crossing a border accomplish? If we managed to survive through sheer chance, where would we end up? Was there even such a thing as a better choice? I still couldn't understand the purpose of this fight for survival. I caught Haemin's eyes - he was watching us through the car window, his face pressed against the glass. He wasn't crying, even without his mum and dad next to him. He looked at us blankly, still looking a little sleepy, like he was watching a cartoon. He rubbed his eyes and picked his nose.

—It's fine.

I said under my breath as I got back in the car. I opened the rear door and pulled Haemin into my arms, aware of the eyes watching us from behind curtains.

—It's fine. This is just how life is.

I rubbed Haemin's back, trying to convince myself as much as him.

—Mum, I need to pee.

Haemin squirmed against me. Protecting what deserved protection, avoiding what should be avoided, not trusting anyone too easily. Feeling ashamed when I did something wrong. Questioning why I was still breathing today. That had been life in Korea. Life here wasn't so different. No – it was different. Here I could focus on the people I loved. I could truly observe them, listen to them, treasure their words and gestures. I couldn't manage that in Korea. I had put precious people on hold. Because there would always be tomorrow. Because we could reconnect later. Because we assumed we had endless time ahead of us. That was no longer the case.

I stepped out and wrapped my coat around Haemin. He walked into a narrow alley and hesitated before lowering his trousers.

—Don't look.

—Okay, I won't.

I turned away but couldn't help glancing back over my shoulder. Haemin's stream hit the building wall, sending up little puffs of steam in the cold air. His body heat. He waved me over. I waited a beat, pretending I hadn't been watching, then walked over and pulled him into a hug. He wriggled a little, embarrassed, but he didn't push me away. I had to protect him. I couldn't forget what it meant to be human – not anymore. The next time Haemin asked when we were going home, I'd have to give him a real answer. I'd have to explain as best I could. No more putting things off. I had to tell him the truth: *I love you.*

Dori

For days I lay in the remote warehouse with a blanket over my face. I fell into a deep sleep but kept jerking awake. Couldn't pull myself together. My mouth stayed dry, no matter how much snow I boiled and drank. I wanted to talk to Joy, but my eyes kept closing. Couldn't fight it off no matter how hard I tried. Whether it was sleep or death, I couldn't tell.

I was scared. What if I'd caught the disease that took Mum? My mental anguish far exceeded any physical symptoms. Fear was like a large hand gripping me by the throat, dragging me somewhere close to death. I wanted to make a deal. If there were anything left in my life that could be exchanged for death, I would gladly give it up, whatever it was. Despite doing everything to survive, I was still preoccupied with death. I was too busy thinking about why we die, why we had to die, why we have to die, and what comes after death, that I didn't think to think about life. I was wrapped up in thoughts like, *If Joy dies, I'll—, If I died, Joy will—*. I shouldn't have done that. I needed to live in the moment. I should've left future matters for the future.

Faintly, I could make out Joy peering down at me. She rummaged through my rucksack and took out our last tinned items. Two tins of beans from the woman on the road. Joy boiled the tins in melted snow and spooned a few beans into my mouth at a time. I gagged but held it in. She fed me slowly, patiently, persistently.

I opened my eyes.

Joy was nowhere in sight.

My mind became as clear and cold as the winter sky. My limbs ached but didn't feel heavy. I walked out of the door and looked for footprints. Everything had been erased by the relentless snow. I couldn't reach Joy once she was out of sight; she wouldn't hear no matter how loudly I called out to her. I stood completely still, listening. I could only hear clumps of snow falling from trees. I couldn't tell whether it was about to be sunset or sunrise. I couldn't even tell how long I'd slept. But on the verge of death or not, I'd know if someone had taken Joy. I'd know even from the grave. If Joy had walked out herself, if I were Joy . . . I looked around. Near the warehouse there was a house with all its windows broken. I pulled out the revolver and opened the front door. I searched the house, but she wasn't there. I stepped through the fence gate and stood in the middle of the road. Wooden houses were packed together on either side.

I felt utterly alone in the world.

Something not unlike loneliness. That ridiculous feeling I tried to brush aside, the dread clinging to me like white lint on a black shirt. I was sick of being scared. It had become part of me. Where did everyone go? How did the world become so empty of people? Looking left and right, I still couldn't decide which way to go. I felt like I'd grow further from Joy whichever way I went. I decided to count to a hundred first. One hundred passed in no time. I counted to one hundred again. I anxiously looked around. The day was getting darker. Holding onto the fence, I started along the path on the right. I reached a street corner after six houses. There, I turned around. My tiny angel was at the end of the road, approaching with quick, short steps. I ran over to her. I fell over multiple times. Joy looked surprised, wiping her face with her sleeves. When I started crying, she held out her arms and hugged me.

Joy took out dried corn kernels and a lighter from her coat pocket. Plus dry pasta wrapped in paper. She said she'd found them in a vacant house on the corner. There was more food to bring over. The house wasn't big, but a book collection lined the walls and kept the house warm.

—Don't ever go off on your own again.

Joy watched my lips intently.

—I can't just sit around while you're in pain.

—But still. Don't go off on your own.

—I can handle this sort of thing now.

I signed back with big, slow motions.

—Don't leave me alone. That's what I mean.

There really were a lot of books. And a wide desk too. I looked through each book filled with unrecognisable letters. I'd hoped to find a map but didn't. No dictionary either. If I could read the shopfronts and signposts, if I could understand the language, we'd be safer. We should head to the city once my health improved. We had to find a bookshop. My mind was slightly put at ease now that I had a goal. I had motivation.

After laying out our blankets and sleeping bags under the large desk, I told Joy to get some sleep. I found a bucket in the back garden and collected some snow. I made a fire and melted the snow in the kitchen with wide windows. I wetted some pages in warm water and wiped the blood left on my skin. There was dried blood all over my thighs, chest, stomach, shoulders and armpits. Joy crawled out of her sleeping bag and leant against the doorframe, watching me without a word.

—Don't worry. I'm not in pain. Go to sleep.

Actually, I was in pain. My whole body ached. I was barely managing to move.

—What did we do wrong?

I pondered her question.

—Joy. If someone tries to hurt you, don't stay still.

I tried to convey my message as slowly as possible. If I said I hadn't seen it coming, of course that would be a lie. I'd put up my guard the moment we stepped inside that box van. I wasn't family. I was just some woman they'd picked up. Some of them would blatantly look me up and down when Jina wasn't next to me. A look of contempt and superiority. They always wore this belittling expression as they brushed up against me to intimidate me. It made me feel . . . like vermin. They acted like I was unworthy, seeing nothing but my sex. I'd tried my best not to engage them by talking or making eye contact. I'd strived to hide my existence.

Joy looked deep in thought.

—I thought everything was good because we were getting a ride, and Geonji and Jina were there.

So had I. The good things had been so close to us, growing bigger and bigger until they covered the bad things.

—That's my fault.

I held out my thumbs and index fingers and turned them outward.

—It's not wrong to feel good about something.

—I didn't know that you were getting hurt. I was asleep. That's my fault too. I don't know anything when I close my eyes.

—None of this is your fault. Stop arguing and go to sleep already.

Making an anguished face, Joy tucked herself into her sleeping bag. *I'll follow your orders. I don't eat that much either. I'll sleep only a little. I'll do anything you say* . . . Those phrases popped into my head. Maybe they were from a book or a film. I was struck with the humiliation and discomfort I'd felt when I'd first encountered them. Once I recalled them, I kept remembering them as if under a spell. I said them aloud to expel them. They didn't roll off the tongue. Joy was intentionally making things her fault. It was possible we needed that strategy to understand our situation and accept the parting. But I felt uneasy.

That night, I dreamt about Yeonu. I was looking for her at some kind of night market. Amid the crowd of people eating and drinking and shouting, I caught glimpses of the yellow school bag she always used to wear. I called out to her, but she didn't turn around. In order to reach Yeonu I had to cut across a group of middle-aged men boozing and playing with hwatu cards. The men didn't let me pass. I tripped on something. A doorsill, a jagged rock, a foot, I couldn't tell. The thought of Yeonu tripping on the same thing filled me with rage. But in the dream, I couldn't let it out. My screaming produced no sounds, and swinging my fists only drew mocking laughter. After walking around and around the maze-like market, I found an empty lot that had been swept by sandy winds. The blue light of dawn hung in the air. Yeonu approached me on an old scooter. I played it cool to hide the feelings tightening inside my chest. Suddenly we were somewhere else. Yeonu and I were walking on the beach near sunset. The tide was out so it was muddy. There were a lot of people around. Against the evening sun, strong and cast low in the sky, they looked dark like shadows. Dark seagulls hovered. I was annoyed by the wind messing up my hair. I wanted to look nice in front of Yeonu. She was walking ahead when she stooped to pick something up from the mudflat. It was a small note with heavily blurred text. We looked at it closely. Yeonu held up the note.

—I lost this a really long time ago.

—Where did you lose it?

—The day I moved to a new house. It flew away in the wind.

—But it's here now?

—After wandering round and round.

—How did it get here?

—The way we did.

Yeonu's hand trembled a bit. I leaned closer.

—What does it say?

With a flurry of wind, the note flew away.

Did I dream about Yeonu because of that book Jina had given me, *Annam*?

I peered into the darkness.

Will we wander round and round and meet again?

Yeonu used to shelve books in the school library. Sometimes I pushed the trolley with her. Between the less-frequented shelves in the two-hundred or three-hundred section, we could be left to ourselves for hours. We existed in a time of our own in that quiet, warm space. I'd demanded a promise from her back then: *Let's never get married, not even when we're older. Since we can't marry each other, promise me you won't do anything with someone else that you can't do with me.* I didn't want to imagine Yeonu holding hands or kissing or whispering secrets with her cheek pressed against someone other than me. My own imagination turned me against her. I threw a fit whenever I sensed Yeonu drifting away while fearing my temper would keep us apart. I lashed out in fear then tiptoed around her. *Why are you so precious to me?* I made her miserable with my tantrums. How could I have been so stupid? Was I any different now? Was I living differently? Once we started at different universities, we talked less often and broke up without saying much – but I never forgot about Yeonu. Not even a little. My heart beating the way it did meant something. Was Yeonu still alive? Did she see me in her dreams? Did she still want to look nice in front of me, even in a dream?

The light of dawn was making the house appear darker inside. I slipped out of my sleeping bag and took another quick look at the books on the shelf before grabbing Jina's gift from my rucksack. I walked to the window and opened *Annam* to a random page:

> *The winter lasted months and months. Only in May did the sun appear.*

I couldn't *not* think about Jina, but I didn't want to think about Jina. Studying my reflection in a small mirror, I took off my woolly hat. I touched my hair, tangled and matted with dried blood.

You said you'd give me a nice little bob.

If Jina were here, she'd say, *Let's wait till it's bright outside.* She'd tell me to go rinse my hair with warm water. Make me wait until my hair was dry enough to brush it neatly. With a pair of scissors she'd cut my hair slowly and carefully, making sure the ends were even. I imagined her doing it while looking at my reflection. I picked up the jackknife. I grabbed a handful of hair and snipped it off like weeds. I cut off all the clumps of blood, tousled my hair, and put my hat back on. I picked up the hair that had fallen to the floor and threw it in the dying fire.

The snow stopped. My fears vanished. Perhaps they'd been replaced by resignation. If I could set anything aside, I wanted to set some of my worries aside. If I stayed alive, spring would come. How many days had we been in Russia? I had no idea. I asked Joy; she shrugged. February 9th was her birthday. Since we'd left Korea in December, her birthday could be coming up soon. It could've passed already. I should've counted the days.

I held Joy's hand.

We walked north towards the river.

Jina

I didn't want to speak at all, so I didn't.

I couldn't stop obsessing over Dori's last question. Why had I shaken my head? I thought brooding would make the reason clearer, but it kept slipping further away instead.

My aunt's husband fell seriously ill. High fever, diarrhoea, vomiting. We couldn't identify the illness by the symptoms alone. We were all terrified he'd caught the virus. No one dared go near him. After suffering from visual and auditory hallucinations, he died without proper care. My aunt, alone in her wailing and rage, grabbed my father's gun, put it in her mouth, and pulled the trigger. The ground and river were frozen solid, so we couldn't bury them. We left their bodies in the forest.

At a dip in the road, the box van ahead launched into the air and crashed. A tyre blew. The van spun out of control and tumbled downhill. My uncle at the wheel and my cousin beside him died on impact. We dragged their bodies between the dense trees and buried them in snow.

*

One box van. Six of us left. A paternal uncle, a maternal uncle, a paternal aunt and her husband, my father and me. My despair and helplessness from this strange virus had dulled. We could die not from disease or bandits, but from a car accident or thirst. We could turn guns on each other. Father worried only about fuel. The petrol drum grew lighter each day. Fewer cars and people appeared on the road.

Father said he'd find fuel in a big city and drive us to Moscow. He'd set his mind on scouting the western border before crossing. I wanted to ask why we had to keep moving. He dismissed staying put as if it were cursed. Endless asphalt, cracked and buckled, cut through the empty plains. The box van nearly flipped countless times. No one flinched at the swaying anymore. We'd grown so numb I thought we'd die without noticing.

Was Geonji making his way to some warm beach? When we first met, Dori said she was heading towards the sunset. Was she still travelling that direction? When spring comes, the earth and rivers will thaw; the world will turn green. Flowers will bloom, the sun will shine, berries will ripen. Nature will continue its course, unchanged by human gunfire and destruction and slaughter. I wanted to stay and welcome spring. I wanted to live somewhere with trees and flowers and clear rivers, not knowing if I was human or wind. I wanted to meet someone who understood shame.

*

Beyond a village of small houses, a winding mountain road appeared. Past the mountain and a frozen reservoir lay another similar village. We spotted a concrete city in the distance. I could tell it was massive before we reached it. A major city, ruthlessly destroyed. Heaps of shattered concrete, building remnants scattered like paper scraps . . . It made no sense. These ruins seemed impossible without heavy artillery or earthquakes. I'd seen countless abandoned or torched houses, but never this kind of devastation – concrete buildings pulverised as if a giant had stomped through. Did the bandits here have tanks and artillery? After studying the scene through his binoculars, Father leapt down from the van roof and steered towards a secluded path. He'd spotted dozens of tanks, rising flames and people moving in groups. He decided to hide in the mountains and observe for a little longer.

Soon after, we watched a convoy of military lorries approach the city entrance. It stretched like a long train loaded with people, cargo and weapons. Artillery I'd only seen in films. People who didn't look like soldiers transporting military equipment. Where were they taking these terrifying things? Where had these people come from? Something was happening, something unprecedented. We hadn't realised how narrowly we'd escaped danger all along. The worst possibilities could have been stalking us the entire time. Watching the convoy charge forward, I couldn't stop thinking: If we'd arrived moments later or moved slightly faster, they would have caught us. They might not have harmed us. They might have given us positions behind their artillery instead of targeting us with it.

But I didn't want to be behind or in front of any artillery. I wanted to get as far from those things as possible.

Father was convinced war would break out. The nation has started mobilising, he said, mentioning the nuclear weapons within its borders. He insisted we cross the border before more time passed. He unfolded the map and located the nearest crossing. I couldn't understand him. What did he mean by 'nation' in this ruined world? Or 'military'? If such institutions existed, we never could have left Korea. These were bandits masquerading as soldiers. If he was right - if nuclear weapons dotted this land and these fake soldiers had seized them - we should flee north, not south or west. We should hide in the mountains and live like animals. But he was adamant. He claimed we could reach the border in under a day if we drove without stopping. He emptied the remaining fuel from the drum into the petrol tank.

When darkness fell, Father climbed on top of the box van again and observed the city through his binoculars. He sounded possessed when he climbed down.

—They have electricity. They're using electricity. Lights in the buildings, streetlights too.

This meant a power plant was running. That was

tempting. With electricity we'd suffer less from hunger and cold. My aunt's husband spoke up.

—Where are we going?

Father wouldn't look at us. He fiddled with his binoculars.

—We need to move.

—Where?

—Something's not right.

Father muttered before settling into the driver's seat.

—Where the hell is he trying to take us? He should explain himself.

Grumbling, my aunt stepped into the cargo hold. The box van quietly entered the road.

Loaded like freight, we had travelled across more than half of Russia. Initially, there wasn't enough space in the cargo hold, packed with petrol drums and supply boxes. We had to secure them with heavy rope to prevent them from crushing us. When we lay on our sleeping bags, the cacophony of breathing, sleep talking and snoring floated around us like dust. Now the cargo space was nearly empty. Food and fuel ran out faster than anticipated. People died from unexpected causes. On the road, my relatives shot strangers whose faces and names meant nothing to them. They abandoned Geonji. And Dori, they . . . Wherever we finally settled, we'd spend the rest of our lives carrying wounds from this journey. We might have to accept our survival not as a miracle but as a heavy burden to bear.

*

Gunshots erupted from every direction. The box van lurched until it tipped onto its side. Bullets punched through the cargo hold. The box van slowed abruptly, then stopped. My aunt collapsed into a corner and lost consciousness. My maternal uncle tried to open the cargo door, but my paternal uncle-in-law blocked him. My uncle shoved my uncle-in-law aside.

—If we don't get out, we'll be shot full of holes.

The door opened. Eerie silence greeted us outside. Beyond the door stretched a vast field. I sensed bloodlust in the silence.

—Let . . . let's turn ourselves in. No, sur, surrender . . .

Gunshots silenced him. More bullets pierced the cargo hold in rapid bursts; my uncle-in-law collapsed. Gunmen surrounded the door, weapons aimed at us. We placed our hands on our heads and exited the box van. Father and his younger brother were bound and forced prone on the asphalt like dead frogs. My maternal uncle was killed while emptying his clip on the run. My aunt and I were thrown onto the cold ground. The gun muzzle, hard and terrifying, pressed against the back of my head.

The gunmen replaced and repaired our tyres on the spot. They confiscated all our weapons and ammunition and transferred our few remaining supplies to their own lorry. Then they took turns raping my aunt and me. I heard gunfire and screeching brakes, screaming and crying. While others attempting to reach the border were beaten and robbed and killed and captured, I was repeatedly assaulted. The distant red glow swelled beyond the horizon. Ghostly sounds rode the wind, but I felt no cold. The moon, white and round, rose peacefully to shine down on us. As if someone were watching from the sky. As if they reclined in a cosy armchair by the fire, observing all this unfold over strong coffee and walnut pie. I wanted to ask: *How many times have you watched this scene? Why won't you turn it off?* I wanted to flip the sky over like a table. The bandits controlled the road until sunrise, plundering anyone and anything that tried to pass. There was no life left in Father's eyes. Even as he stared at me, he did not see me.

The gunmen's chatter and laughter never stopped during the robberies and murders. How could they laugh? Were they making jokes? What kind of humour was appropriate in this situation? Was it anything like the jokes we'd shared while roasting lamb over a campfire? I remembered Dori's silent gaze as she watched me laugh when we first met. Her dark eyes had sparked with surprise. How did she not slap my face? How did she simply watch me without cursing or spitting? The box van began moving. Collapsed in the cargo hold like a slaughtered pig, I was being driven to some unknown destination. I hoped to never see Dori and Geonji again. Wherever I was headed, I hoped not to encounter a familiar face.

Dori

—We'll look for a dictionary and a map once we reach a big city.

—Then?

—Then we decide where to go.

—You said we're looking for summer.

—Summer will come without us looking for it.

—Then why did you say that?

—Because it was cold.

—It's still cold.

—It is.

—Is this country really big?

—Yeah. Really big.

—Will we not see the same people again?

—Probably not.

—Is everyone headed in different directions?

—I don't know.

—They'll punish Geonji.

—Are you worried?

—I have you, but he lost his whole family.

— . . . He has Jina.

—Jina is with bad people.

—That's not entirely true.

—We should've left together.

—With Jina?

—Geonji.

—Do you miss him?

—I'm worried about him. That he'll be alone.

Would we see Geonji again? Probably not. I didn't want to harbour hope about seeing anyone again. I'd almost died several times. Death circled me, not yet having found a way to swallow me whole.

—I was really scared when you were sick. Without you, I'm alone.

—That's not true.

—Without me, you're alone too.

—That won't happen.

—That's why I went outside. To see what I could do on my own.

—Now that you know, don't go off alone again.

These experiences had caused seismic shifts in Joy's heart. Jumbled everything inside. I was hurting after being beaten and chased by the very people we'd travelled with. That . . . that was different from being attacked by strangers on the road. So many questions must have crossed Joy's mind as I lay dying in that warehouse. My heart sank just imagining them.

—I want you to get married.

With that, Joy pivoted to something completely unexpected.

—I don't want you to be alone.

Which is to say, my little angel didn't think or act like me.

—I want there to be three of us, not two. Four would be even better.

She'd been pretending to be fine while her mind raced with fear. Not about where we should go next, but how we could be fine here and now.

—You liked being with Jina and Geonji.

—Yeah, because I learnt we can live differently with people like them.

—Good things don't last forever.

—I know.

— . . .

—I learnt something.

—That you can like people?

—That I get lonely when I lose something I like.

— . . .

—If you get married, you don't have to go separate ways.

—You can separate even if you're married.

—Stupid. You know that's not what I mean.

Joy hit her chest and sighed. She stared at the blue sky, choosing her words, then wrapped her little finger around mine.

—I'm telling you to make a promise.

White breath streamed from her mouth.

—Promise you won't separate no matter what. When you get married, you promise to stay together forever . . .

I stroked her shoulder.

—You can separate even if you promise. People are like that.

—You're not nice.

Joy's eyes filled with resentment.

—You make everything hard by only saying mean things.

She stomped ahead, shoulders shaking. Not crying, just huffing with anger. I ran after her.

—Then will you marry me?

I smiled as I said it.

—Why would I marry you?

Joy was serious.

—We don't need that. We don't need promises. You're stupid.

She was so angry I stopped smiling.

—If you promise someone, and I promise someone, we'll be four. The four that'll never ever part.

—Okay, fine.

—I'm scared it's just us two.

—I'm scared too.

I hugged Joy. I didn't want to be cruel. I didn't want to say *That's just how people are*. But didn't we need to believe that to survive, to keep going? What had I grown up hearing? *It's a dog-eat-dog world. Don't trust anyone. Being nice makes you weak. Don't look desperate. Survival of the fittest. Every man for himself. Winner takes all.* I'd heard it all long before the virus spread. Even people who criticised these ideas repeated them. Those things I told Joy to keep her safe – were they stopping her from dreaming? Was I limiting her to barely surviving, like me? *But Joy, we weren't the ones who left. We didn't abandon them. I wanted to stay together, I wanted to promise* . . . I pushed these thoughts away. Later, when I was stronger, I could examine them.

At every village, we searched empty houses for food. We met elderly people who'd stayed behind – those who believed they could recover in the spring with sun and land. They knew the local geography, lived off provisions from mountains and rivers. They gave all thanks to God . . . The young people must've either died or left. If they were passionate, if they believed in more days ahead, if they still hungered for untasted happiness, they had no choice but to leave. Was the virus still mutating? I'd heard that even vaccines couldn't keep up with the mutation rate. Someone must still be working on it. That's what humans do, we carry strange burdens like duty and responsibility. There must be people fighting alone, determined to save the world from waste. And others turning this disaster into a festival of murder and madness. I have both responsibility and madness in me. I can't say the two are mutually exclusive.

I grew dizzy and breathless quickly. We rested often and didn't rush.

More abandoned villages appeared as we neared the city. Snow came down hard again.

Geonji

If I'd seen this coming, I would've run off with Dori.

No, wait. Then I wouldn't have had a chance to say goodbye to Jina.

And I can't let Jina down.

My feelings weren't hurt or anything. I have complicated feelings about her dad, but the other adults were practically foaming at the mouth, screaming to get me out. What else could he do? His younger brother had just been killed . . . All I wanted to know was whether he'd taken part too. Did Jina's dad draw a number and wait his turn to rape Dori? Or did he just look the other way, knowing exactly what was happening? He had to have known. The front door was right there in his line of sight. I respected Jina's dad like I respected her mum. If I respected her as much as King Sejong the Great, then I respected him as much as Lee Seung-yuop, king slugger of the Samsung Lions. When he hit Dori, I was surprised but not betrayed. I mean, I took note that he could snap too. There's no one I should avoid more than someone who gets violent when they're mad. Everything

I thought I knew was falling apart. Would he have hit me too, if I'd tried to stop him?

I don't know.

Jina had slipped me some food. She cried so hard I thought she might pass out. It didn't feel like goodbye forever. There was no way that'd be the last time I'd see her.

When Mum died, I was completely torn up with anger and grief. It felt like *I* was dying. That's when I cut myself off from the world. I hated everything and turned my back on it all. When my old man died . . . I'd always wanted him dead, but when it actually happened, I felt something I couldn't understand. I felt bad for him. And because I couldn't forgive myself for feeling sorry for that asshole, I locked myself in Jina's shed and punished myself. But when I saw Jina about to leave in that box van, I realised something about myself, like what really mattered to me. No matter how much I hurt myself, there was this thing inside me that was different – a different world from what my parents showed me. It was the world Jina showed me, the one she made for me. Because of her, I didn't have to turn out exactly like them. I thought I'd just die the second she left, and I was fine with that. I was ready to gulp down whatever life I had left like poison. But Jina came shrieking and pulled me out. She saved me. So how could I love anyone else? How could I live in a world without Kwon Jina? We're bound to meet again. After all the years I spent in silence, getting hit and never really acting out, I think God could spare me this one piece of luck. Don't you think, God?

According to the map Jina's dad studied every day, there were lots of routes to Africa. I could go through Kazakhstan and the Middle East, or through Europe. I missed my phone. If I could just check Google Maps, I'd know where I was, the quickest route, what was happening in the world . . . No, I wouldn't. Like the internet would even work now, idiot. When I was little, I saw this book at the library – *Travel the World on Foot* or something. I should've read it. Back then I didn't give a damn about the world, much less travel. Just meaningless words to me. I was obsessed with the *Absolute Dominion* martial arts webtoon by Jang Yeong-hoon. Jeok Lee-Geon's world – where he took down evil one by one and knew what it meant to be a good adult – felt more real to me than anything else. Anyway, even though I never read that travel book, I figure I can make it on foot as long as the title wasn't total bullshit. I can travel the world. I just can't walk across the Pacific Ocean.

I walked with my back to the sun. It crept up, then cut right in front of me. Winter winds lashed at my body. Back in Korea, I'd been alone even when surrounded by people. Had to read every room, watch for every reaction. Not anymore. Now I just had to be true to myself. As I walked alone, my mind started racing. I wanted to prepare for the future but kept getting stuck on the past. *That happened, oh right, and there was that person – I'd totally forgotten. You were such an idiot back then. Be brave now, be righteous. Who's going to recognise your bravery out here alone? Practice anyway. Become a better person.*

When you see Kwon Jina again, you'll be a good adult. No, don't think, you're wasting energy. Survive first, don't think, save your energy . . . I ran through these resolutions as I walked, listing and crossing them out again and again.

I thought of my uncle – Mum's brother, more than ten years younger than her. I barely had any memories of him. He was always off backpacking somewhere. Wherever he liked, he'd just stay and make it work doing whatever job he could find – kitchen assistant, janitor, manual labourer, mover, tour guide. In Korea, people looked down on him for taking those kinds of jobs, and he'd get angry when anyone treated him like crap. But he said it felt totally different abroad. If people ignored him, he ignored them back. Even when things got tough, he didn't get depressed and kept his confidence. Being young was a burden in Korea, but freedom everywhere else. I'd heard all this at my grandmother's funeral. She'd been sick for so long, basically dying for almost a year. My uncle came back and she died right after. Mum held onto him and cried. All the adults badgered him: *How much longer will you loaf around? You need to settle down, make money, get married.* Where was he now? The virus had to have hit wherever he was too. If we met again somewhere out here, would we even recognise each other? Or would we just run, draw weapons, seeing only another stranger . . . I felt so empty. Everyone had died. People who found good jobs in their twenties and worked hard to build their futures. People like my uncle who threw themselves into whatever they enjoyed without worrying about money or marriage. People like my old man who tortured themselves by torturing others. People like Mum who felt sorry for people like him and lived with depression their whole lives . . . They were all dead. Why was *I* still alive? No. I didn't want to assign a reason for why I was still alive. Then there'd be a reason Mum died, and I couldn't accept that. If the bunkers were real, and they were occupied by people living honourably during this disaster, then what kind of people were they? If they were to repopulate Earth, would they create a different world?

I don't want to go anywhere that resembles a bunker.
I don't want to survive among people in a place like that.
I'm going to survive quietly. Protect the good things until I die.
Good things are precious. What makes me who I am.

This is what I decided to do.

Roads simply connected village after village. Occasional cars passed. Sometimes, I caught the faint sound of gunshots. Black smoke curled from a faraway field. I paused, wondering if I'd find people there. Was it right, to go where people were? I had to decide for myself. That's what it meant to be alone. I retraced my steps. Darkness fell. I hurried, desperate to find shelter. I spotted a village not too far away with small houses huddled together. Suddenly, this cold fear washed over me. I had to spend the night alone. My safety was a gamble with or without villagers. I carried no gun or knife, had never really fought anyone. I didn't even know how to make a proper fist. At the village entrance, I rushed into the first place with four walls and a roof. I held my breath and listened. My heart was beating too loudly. I scanned the whole place with a torch. Broken furniture, shattered windows, sunken floor. I set a display cabinet upright to blockade the door, then sat on a ripped sofa. Listening to fierce winds, I waited for my fear to calm. I tried to remember what Dori and Jina had done when we were together. I went outside to gather some dry branches and searched the house for paper to use as kindling. I brought a large basin from the bathroom and made a small fire inside it. I watched the flame spew soot. I caught myself muttering, *You have to get used to this.* Alarmed by my voice, I shut my mouth. My eyes kept closing, but I was too scared to fall asleep. I laid out my sleeping bag on the sofa and wrapped myself in a blanket. Every single one of the promises I'd made during the day suddenly felt absurd.

I opened my eyes.

It was bright all around.

For a moment I couldn't tell what was going on. I slowly went back through what happened yesterday. Then I went over everything, trying to make sense of it all. My mind gradually cleared. The cabinet I'd used to blockade the door was still there. My rucksack next to me. Nothing had happened overnight. I didn't die, wasn't robbed. I'd slept, and now it was morning. It felt like I'd accomplished something huge, maybe the most important thing in my life.

—Good morning.

I said it in English, the way Jina and I always did, to nobody. Pride hit me hard, made my chest feel tight and full. Calmly, I looked out of the window, started a fire to heat up a tin of sweetcorn, and ate it. I dumped everything out of my rucksack. I had to know exactly how much I had of what. I scoured the house, but didn't find a single thing to eat. Instead, in a desk drawer, I found a small box of matches and a rusted pocket knife. The knife was only as short as my index finger, but it was better than nothing. I also took a pen and a small notepad with Russian letters on the first few pages, followed by many more blank ones. I needed to leave a record. Because I was alone, because no one would ever know or remember me as I was in that moment, I wanted to at least keep a simple record of what I saw and ate, what happened as I walked. If only for someone to discover my record if I died. If only to have someone remember my handwriting.

I put on my rucksack and headed out. I had a splitting headache and my skin felt like it was about to crack, but the cold air was refreshing. I wandered around the village, looking through each house. Some were burned down, but six or seven were still standing. I found signs that someone had stayed in one recently. Could've been last night, could've been a few days ago. Either way, someone was here. Were they alone? Did they have company? Were they still alive? Would we end up going the same way?

Maybe it was the sun, but I wasn't overly scared like last night.

I was going to wake up safe and say good morning to Jina every day. I was going to stack my precious days, walking all the way to a warm ocean . . . I felt like I'd just opened a forty-five-volume martial arts series I'd been putting off for years.

Real life started now.

Jina

The sun rose as we entered the city.

So many buildings destroyed. Lorries and freight cars huddled in packs. Red flags fluttered with text I couldn't read. People moved in lines with their hands on their heads while armed men watched. More lorries loaded with people like chickens headed to slaughter. We were let out in front of a large circular building surrounded by a church, shops and a low-rise apartment complex. The armed men divided us into men and women. They didn't yell or beat us into submission. Instead, with a shot to the head, they promptly executed whoever didn't follow orders or showed the slightest hesitation. They herded the women into a large building with high ceilings and no windows. It might've been a supermarket once. Several men came in, did a cursory health check on us, and asked our country of origin and age in English and Russian. They stood to attention when a man wearing clean clothes and a healthy glow walked in the door. As he spoke, the armed man standing next to him interpreted his words into English.

—We saved you from death's grip . . . You can now serve in this war. It is an honourable battle. A sense of responsibility and duty is essential. You will be rewarded based on your achievements. Traitors will pay an irreversible price . . . You are capable of building a city and an encampment. A new world will be created on this land. Dedicate your labour to those fighting on the frontlines. They will protect your lives.

That was all I caught from his lengthy speech. He told those who wished to participate in combat to step forward. A woman raised her hand to say something. A gun went off. The woman was dead. We put our hands on our heads and walked outside single-file. Another gunshot, sudden as the last. I looked back. A woman at the end of the line had fallen. I had no idea why they killed her. Before long we reached a demolished building. Women were already there, carting wheelbarrows, clearing wreckage, collecting rebar. I was assigned a wheelbarrow. Monitored by armed men, we couldn't chat or rest. One of them fired his gun in the air when darkness fell. We returned to the large building, now teeming with women. So many I couldn't count them. They probably couldn't have abducted this many just from the road. Had the virus died down? Otherwise, why keep this many people in one place?

A large cart rolled into the building, filled with tinned food, bread, beverages. Enough to eliminate any need for us to fight each other. I couldn't believe there was this much food left. I'd thought they wouldn't feed us, that they'd just work us until we starved and dispose of our bodies. I had no idea who controlled this city and what their goals were, but if they were giving *us* food, then somewhere people were eating and drinking much better. These tinned foods and dry bread must be what they considered scraps – stuff they wouldn't even touch. I realised why all the villages and cities we'd passed through lay in ruins. Some group had pillaged them, taken everything: food, people. Everyone else on the road had held each other at gunpoint over the scraps this group had left behind.

I fell asleep against the wall and woke to a chilling sensation. A man pointing a gun at me. I got up reflexively. With his gun, he signalled me to follow. Other women were being forced out too. The moment we entered the dilapidated apartment, he took off his trousers. I heard screams from every direction. Two more men entered the apartment overnight. We returned to the large building after sunrise. An incredible amount of food was carted in again. I vomited mid-bite but still finished eating. We lined up and went to work. We finished working, came back, and fought off sleep while eating. Night and day tick-tocked away.

Were they brainwashed?

I looked at the people pulling triggers, unfazed like they were wielding fly swatters.

Could they be choosing this if they were perfectly sane?

I thought back to my father and uncles shooting bandits. He fired his gun even when the bandits were unarmed. I'd closed my eyes and turned away every time. Blocked my ears. I didn't hate my father; I only feared him. I might've died if it hadn't been for him. That's why I couldn't speak up and say, *Do you have to shoot the unarmed too?* Where was he now? Was he alive? My aunt had stopped speaking. We shared the same space but grew further apart. She stopped recognising me.

We rummaged through the wreckage to collect rebar and transport rocks, scooped sand from hills and rivers to carry in sacks, stacked rocks to build trenches, applied cement. Alternating between these tasks, I was gradually forgetting how to think. Memories blurred. Emotions dulled. Past events felt like dreams – not that the present felt real either. People didn't seem like people, and I didn't feel like a person. So I had to reminisce. Whenever I could remember to, I had to remind myself. My name on Dori's lips. Her voice. Her plump earlobes. Joy's eyes. Geonji's dream. All that I desperately wished were still alive. Remembering them, I'd promise myself:

I will not die here.

Not here. Not like this.

I shouldn't forget these sentences, even if they were completely meaningless. I should remember them like my own name.

One night, someone pointed a gun at my forehead after I'd passed out from exhaustion. I opened my eyes. It was Father.

—This was the only way we could meet.

Father spoke as soon as we stepped inside the dilapidated apartment.

—I knew you'd stay alive. Of course. You're my daughter.

He looked well. Healthy complexion, clean haircut and shave. He wore a padded coat, the kind worn by those who dragged me into this apartment every night.

—I told you. It's war.

There was a war between armed groups. Russia alone was overtaken by a dozen factions, while Europe and the Middle East had closed their borders. All the groups used large cities as bases, and the conflict was becoming increasingly violent. When the strongest group took over Russia, that would become the new Russia. New Russia would swallow Mongolia, even Kazakhstan.

—We had to subdue the other groups with nukes. We couldn't do it alone, but it was possible with alliances.

Father was clearly excited laying out this information. He wasn't my dad, the man who'd watched me with vacant eyes as we parted.

—We?

—Yes. Everyone fighting here.

—Who's fighting who?

—I've already explained this to you. Just wait it out a little longer, even if it's hard. We can start a new life here.

—*We* who work like slaves every day and get raped every

night? Auntie doesn't even recognise me anymore. *We* say one wrong thing and get our heads blown off.

—But you don't starve here, right? You can live as long as you follow orders. Good days will come if you wait. We could be rulers of a new nation.

—Dad.

—I was on the southern frontline. I protected the border. You have no idea how many people I killed.

Father looked down at his hands.

—That's how much I've contributed. This is how we'll survive. It's far better than starving to death on the streets. You have no idea how intense the battle is. You'll die like a dog the minute you leave this place.

—Dad, I'm already a dog here. A dog.

—You just have to change your perspective. Don't think of yourself as a victim. We're all fighting on the same side.

—So you're fine with this?

—I see how the world works. There's a rumour Korea's already been invaded by Chinese gangs.

—Is there nothing more to the world than what *you've* seen?

—No news goes unheard around here. I can't live wandering the roads again. Having people on your side, being able to rely on them, that's good. Everyone here is on the same side.

—Dad, you have to pretend to rape me every time we meet. Are you saying you're fine with this?

—We have to get used to it. Brace ourselves. Once I

rise in the ranks, I can get you out of here. You'll live like a princess. We'll even get a house of our own. I'm doing all kinds of terrible things for you. I'll be recognised for my efforts.

—While others remain trapped.

—You'll get out soon. It won't take long. Just trust me.

—Dad, I'm going to die before then.

—Don't say that. Have some faith in your dad. It'll all work out. You have no idea what it's like out there.

—I can't stand this.

—Jina.

Father held my face. His hands were shaking. He was struggling to contain his anger.

—Don't look at me like that. I'm not the bad guy.

—I know. You love me, Dad. You don't need to convince me.

—There's no other way. Here, if you don't pick up a gun, you do manual labour. Then you lose out. I'll be recognised for my contributions, and I *will* keep you safe.

—I don't want anything from you. You're struggling to survive, just like me. So don't tell me it'll get better. Don't say everyone here is on the same side. How can you call that hope?

—Jina.

—Don't act like you're doing something good. Don't call this an opportunity. Don't say you're doing your best. Please.

Father was dreaming a new dream. This dream was so

intense, so enormous, that it crushed my dad, the man who used to call after me if I was out of his sight for even a moment. This new man, who told me to wait it out a little longer because I haven't starved or died, had defeated my old dad. And so his war had begun.

Ryu

Dan and I went back and forth about whether to abandon the car. He couldn't bring himself to leave it behind. When I couldn't convince him, I agreed we'd stay in the city for now. We settled on the second floor of a ten-storey concrete building, an old office space with desks and cabinets toppled everywhere. We stacked the furniture into makeshift walls and flipped over a large bookcase to use as a bed. The next day, Dan hauled in an old mattress from another floor. After two days of searching all ten floors, we'd found a bag of flour, dried apples and hot chocolate mix. The moment I found marshmallows, jellies and biscuits tucked inside a metal desk drawer on the fifth floor, I couldn't help myself. 'Thank you,' I said out loud. I used to keep chocolate in my desk at the travel agency. On days when consultation calls ran back-to-back, my hands would shake and my anemia would act up. I'd eat some chocolate and drink way too much instant coffee. Nothing else could pull me through like that. Did someone still in Seoul go through my desk and find that chocolate? Did they whisper their own prayer of thanks? Haemin tried a marshmallow and smiled – the brightest I'd seen from him in weeks.

The building, with its blown-out windows, looked like a demon riddled with gaping holes. At night, silence took on different shapes, trapping me in my own anxious thoughts. I held Haemin close each time. When I wrapped my arms around him, I was really holding myself together. Even with Dan and Haemin right there beside me, it felt like we were drifting in some distant universe – sharing warmth and worry through touch alone, but nothing deeper. A place where we could only embrace our own private fears and pain.

—Mum.

Haemin had been sucking on a jelly when he placed something small in my palm. I stared at it for a long moment, even though I knew exactly what it was. I examined his mouth. There was an empty space next to his incisor. I touched his gum with my finger. I could feel his permanent tooth growing in.

—When did it start getting loose?

Haemin shrugged.

—I dunno.

—It was wiggly before it fell out, wasn't it?

—I dunno.

—Didn't it hurt?

—Dunno. It just fell out.

I stared at his baby tooth. Even under these circumstances, Haemin kept growing. Getting taller by the day, his body changing in ways I could barely track. He had so much life ahead of him. I closed my fist around the tooth, knowing I needed to keep it safe but worrying about losing something so impossibly small.

Once Haemin was asleep, I showed Dan the tooth. He looked at it for a moment.

—Should we go back to Korea?

—That's where we came from. Did you forget? All those lunatics hunting children for their livers.

—Things might have changed by now. Let's go back and see, start over there. We know Korea. We can figure out how to survive.

What exactly was he trying to start over? Haemin was growing right in front of us, even managing to dream.

— . . . By the time we get back to Korea, spring will be here.

—Spring will come to Korea too.

—The journey back could be more dangerous. We don't even have the car anymore. We'd have to walk the whole way.

—We still need to go somewhere.

—We didn't abandon everything and come all this way here just to turn around.

—Then where do you suggest we go?

—I'm saying we can't go back to Korea. There's nothing left there now, dear.

Something snapped in Dan then.

—You're always like this. You shoot down everything I say. You don't trust me. You just shut me down. That's all you ever do.

I didn't answer. I had no fight in me. We lay there restless, neither of us able to sleep. Was there nowhere in this vast land for us three to hide? Dan got up and paced in the darkness for a while before calling me over to a corner. When I approached, he pushed me down and started pulling at my clothes. I told him I didn't want to. He tried to force himself into me anyway. Our sex life in Korea had followed the same pattern for years: Dan would get up from the couch where he'd been watching TV, come into our bedroom, pull my trousers down, push into me, finish in a couple of minutes, then pull his trousers back up and return to his shows. This happened maybe every other month. No words before or after, no kissing, nothing. It felt like an obligation, like scratching an itch for him. Here in the darkness, it started to hurt, so I pushed him off.

—I'm your husband. Not some animal. Your husband.

I couldn't tell if he was angry or begging.

—I'm going to lose my mind if I don't at least have this. There's nothing else we can do here, honey. Nothing at all.

What he sought was familiarity. The one routine left in this place where everything was strange and terrifying and uncertain. Dan tried to push into me again, and I twisted away. He stared down at me for a moment, then his voice cracked.

—What do we do now? Honey, where do we go? Where can we possibly go?

Tears. Dan was crying. What kind of woman had he loved? Had he ever told *her* that he loved her? Had he truly loved her? Did he still? Did either of us actually know anything about love? My curiosity felt strangely clean – no exhaustion, no shame, no rage, no jealousy. I just wanted to ask him. If he really understood what love was. If he'd ever felt love for someone completely separate from himself, not like our love for Haerim and Haemin.

I stood and pulled my clothes back on. Dan sniffled and did the same.

—What kind of person was she?

He wiped his face and stared at me.

—The woman you were seeing about five years ago.

His face hardened.

—I was going to ask you eventually. How you met her, whether it was serious, why you didn't leave me then. Things like that.

—You knew this whole time and never said anything?

I nodded. He was quiet for a long moment.

—There's not much to tell.

—But tell me anyway. We can talk about this now.

—How could I tell you of all people? I might be a bastard, but . . .

—It doesn't bother me.

—. . .

—You know this about me.

—I don't. I don't know anything. How does this not bother you?

—Because I don't love you.

His face crumpled.

—You don't love me either.

—Why would you say that?

—Honey, we're connected by so many things besides love. We've weathered hard times and made it this far together. If that's love, then fine, it's love, but it doesn't have to be, you know?

— . . .

— . . .

—Still. Don't say that.

—It'll be better than not knowing.

—I don't understand you.

— . . . I want to know.

—You should've asked me back then.

—Back then, I didn't want to know.

—Why not?

—I couldn't afford to.

—So *now* you can?

I let out a laugh.

—Yeah. Now all we have is time.

If we were still in Korea, I wouldn't have been able to ask him this. I might have put it off again and again – until after we'd grown old, after the kids had built their own lives – until

I realised the window had long since closed. Or I might have lashed out at some point before then, surprising us both. I might have screamed, 'How shameless can you be, going out with some woman while I've had to live like this?' Back then, we had so much else demanding our attention: the children's education, our savings, the mortgage, family drama, the gossip and meddling and prejudice of everyone around us . . . Now there was none of that. We only had each other left. We were all we had to focus on. We had to say and hear the things we couldn't before. Once I admitted I didn't love him, I realised those words actually meant nothing. I felt relief at our newfound simplicity. We were Haemin's mum and dad to each other. That was enough.

Dori

In the city, we moved only at night, crouching through its darkest corners. The buildings stood dark, the streets filthy. Sewage everywhere, corpses with missing eyeballs or exposed intestines. Humans hunted dogs and cats for food; dogs and cats fed on human corpses. The day would come when humans ate humans. Someone probably already was. Spring had to come quickly. Rivers and fields had to thaw. Humans might try to drag each other into hell, but nature could slow that descent.

Sometimes I heard the hoarse wail of someone crying, or the ravings of someone gone mad. People wandered the streets like ghosts. I wanted to find a map and a dictionary and get out of the city as fast as possible. We got lost inside a deserted building and found a supermarket that had already been looted. We combed through it anyway. Joy found a box of cereal and some biscuits that had fallen behind a display shelf. We cheered silently, overjoyed. We also found broken candles. But no shoes.

Many buildings had been torched. They actually seemed safer than the intact ones. To escape the wind, we entered a building blackened with soot. I saw firelight deeper inside. Heard voices, too. I grabbed Joy's hand, crept back out and ran without looking back. They might have been good people. We could have helped each other. Or not – that was more likely.

After trudging for a while, we found ourselves in front of a high-rise building. At least thirty storeys tall. Joy pulled at my hand.

—Too big and scary.

We found a smaller building tucked into a corner alley, part of a row of similar structures. I asked Joy if this was okay. She nodded. We hid in the building furthest down the alley. I briefly considered starting a fire but gave up. We ate cold tinned food and waited for daybreak. I fell asleep sitting upright, watching the space slowly fill with light.

Finally, we found a bookshop. Relatively untouched, but still no dictionary. No Russian–Korean, no Russian–English dictionary, not even Russian–Japanese. I couldn't identify the other languages. No map either. Joy picked out a picture book – small and thin, with illustrations but no text. Near the entrance, magazines were scattered around, their pages stiff with cold. My eyes caught on a photo of a red-haired woman in a black cape coat. Only then did I wonder: Why was Jina's hair red? I felt that familiar ache spread through my body, the way it did every time I thought of her. Her beauty had seemed otherworldly from the moment I first saw her, but she had talked to *me*. She had reached for my hand first. That sensation would linger forever, torturing me for the rest of my life. It would make me miss her. It would make me pitiful, the rest of my life dull.

Joy liked the bookshop. We hid there for a day.

We scoured the city for several more days but found no map or dictionary. I didn't feel that sad or desperate. I realised I could make wrong decisions even with a map I could read. What would change by knowing where I was, what lay in every direction? Would I suddenly have a destination? Wouldn't it just confuse me more? Wouldn't I worry and hesitate? If I knew the place I wanted to reach, the place I wanted to avoid, the easy path – I'd probably end up doing what everyone else did. If I knew about walkable routes, I'd only chase those. My knowledge was limited to basics: west was Europe, south was Kazakhstan, farther south was the Middle East, across the Red Sea was Africa. That seemed like enough, and I didn't want to know more. I wanted to stay put, to postpone everything. I wanted to hide somewhere quietly and hibernate like a squirrel.

—Let's go find a library.

—Yeah. Let's.

—Is walking too hard? Are you in pain?

—I'm tired, but it's fine. I can walk.

I managed a slow smile. Her face darkened. Joy's hands moved with quiet insistence.

—No. You need to sleep. Rest today, library tomorrow.

Joy's hand gripped mine tighter. I followed wherever she led me. Just past an old cathedral tucked between low-rise buildings, we hid in a small house buried in shadow. I couldn't bear the chill penetrating my body, so I made a fire. As my body relaxed, I felt the cold even more intensely. The frozen pain thawed and coursed through my entire body like blood. Every breath burned, like glass had shattered in my lungs and heart. My hands, feet and lips trembled so much that I couldn't even get a proper sip of water.

I slept without a single dream.

When I opened my eyes, Joy was massaging my hand.

—How long did I sleep?

She was crying. I reached out to wipe her tears. Her face felt so warm, my hand so cold, that I wondered if I had died. Was I touching Joy after dying without realising it? The thought didn't scare me. I was just relieved to see Joy safe and sound.

—Why are you crying, Joy? Did I sleep too long?

I asked again. If Joy answered, I must still be alive. Wiping her tears, she held up two fingers.

—Two hours?

She shook her head furiously, her shoulders shuddering.

—Two days. Two days without opening your eyes.

Joy must have placed her hand on my heart hundreds of times. I had to get up. I had to show her that her big sister was fine, that her heart was still beating. I pushed myself off the floor and straightened my back. The picture book from the bookshop lay open on the floor. Its blank pages were now filled with Joy's handwriting.

I don't leave my big sister on her own.

My big sister doesn't leave me on my own.

When she wakes up, I'll make a promise.

I'll promise to love her.

Joy would remember me. She was strong and would keep growing. She would become a proper adult. I would grow younger and younger in her memory. One day she would realise: *I thought Dori was an adult back then, but she was only in her early twenties. She was young too.* We need each and every day for that moment to come. We couldn't skip over time.

We slipped out of the small house around sunset. My body hadn't recovered, so I struggled to walk for long stretches. It would take a while to leave this city. I was definitely sick, and though I wouldn't die immediately, I was getting weaker. One day I would become a burden to Joy. Where did I need to go to find Jina? We had parted without making a single promise. *I'll wait for you, let's meet again, I'll come back* . . . We hadn't even said goodbye. Had we met on this frozen land just to become strangers passing by? Was that why we had given ourselves to each other, fallen in love at first sight? Should I not have run away like that? Joy stopped walking and pulled me into a building. I had no strength to resist. Joy signed urgently.

—There's someone over there. Just standing there, watching us.

We peered outside. The sun had set, but it wasn't

completely dark yet. A pale blue light remained. Someone stood at the building entrance across the street, at our ten o'clock, staring at the place we had just been. I took out the gun. I had never fired one. I didn't want to fire one in the future either. I didn't want to kill anyone else.

Wind blew, scattering rubbish. Silent and dark. The person didn't even try to hide, just stared blankly at the ground where we had stood, as if gazing into an untouchable past. A small child emerged from the building and clung to her arm. Only then did I recognise her. I took Joy's hand and walked out to the street. I heard the faint sound of someone crying in the distance. No – the wind? The notes sustained plaintively like a clear, high-pitched aria.

—Do you remember them?

She didn't answer.

—They gave us sweets.

Only then did Joy nod. The woman's husband also came out. The woman slowly waved at us. Our first greeting like that on Russian soil. With the road between us, we watched each other pass.

We could meet like this.

We can meet like this.

If she's alive. As long as she's alive.

A river appeared after we walked for a while. We had followed one to the city, and here we were before a river again. *Back to the starting line.* It was so dark we couldn't see the other side.

—Let's decide in the morning whether to cross.

We entered another low building and made a small fire. Joy fell asleep quickly. I didn't want to think about anything. I was tired. Yet thoughts kept turning towards death. No matter how hard I tried, I could only think about death. I sang to block out the thoughts - sang as softly as I breathed, then closed my mouth. I heard something in the distance. I strained to listen. I couldn't tell what it was. It sounded like thunder, like trains, like the earth splitting. A very heavy sound. I watched Joy sleep as I focused on the sound. Was I losing my mind? I looked out the window but saw only darkness. I stopped myself from dousing the fire and waking Joy. It might be more dangerous to go outside now. I had to find the woman in the morning. I had to ask if she'd heard the same sound. I had to check, through her, whether I was losing my mind. In case something happened to me, I had to ask her to look after Joy. I had to hold onto these fleeting connections. Gripping the revolver, I stared into the darkness and waited for daybreak.

Jina

They kept bringing people over. Killed them as easily as they transported them. A trench surrounded the city. Father said he was going to the border and never came back. Some nights I wasn't dragged to the apartment. I couldn't call myself lucky. What luck was there in any of this? On my way back to the large building after work, I was ordered onto a lorry. People were loaded onto dozens of lorries and driven northeast for hours. Past mountains, a river, fields. Occasionally we spotted villages of small wooden houses and vegetable gardens. The lorries reached a city entrance well after dark. On a field blanketed with snow stood a concrete building, separated from the road by a row of tall, leafless trees. Armed men herded everyone from the lorries into a red cathedral. We would be building an encampment here, they told us. Lorries and tanks loaded with equipment arrived overnight.

Work began at sunrise. We collected corpses lying in the streets and buildings, burnt them with the rubbish. Our work concentrated on the eastern outskirts and around a large river to the west. We hauled dirt, stones and wood from a nearby forest and dug trenches. We filled sunken asphalt and repaired the city. The electricity was promptly restored. There were fewer soldiers than in the last city, which meant less surveillance. In the evening, strangers entered the cathedral – people captured from the road that day. There was a Korean woman among them. She had a child with her. She said her husband had been taken somewhere, but she didn't know where. I told her what I'd been through. She told me what she'd heard from other people on the road: their warnings and laments, their songs. Just being able to talk with her gave me strength. The child cried for his dad. I was afraid the soldiers might kill him for crying.

—Your dad is somewhere here. You'll see him again someday, but only if you don't cry. Let's wait a little. Let's try holding back our tears until we've slowly counted to a hundred in our heads.

I whispered this to the boy, crouching down to his level. Dori had taught me that strategy. To wait until I'd slowly, silently counted to a hundred.

Starting the next day, I never left the woman's side. She never showed her pain or confusion. She worked in silence and ate what she was given. 'I have to find my husband,' she'd said with quiet steel in her voice. So she had to survive this. On the fifth night, she mentioned two sisters. She'd first met them near Baykal and seen them again in this very city not long ago. She never thought she would see them again on this vast land, but they had walked towards her at sunset, like an apparition. The way they walked hand in hand was magical, as pure and moving as a fairytale ending with a happily ever after. Just watching them from a distance had comforted her. They might have been captured and brought here too, but since she hadn't seen them around, they must have escaped to safety . . .

The cathedral doors opened, cutting her off mid-sentence. New captives walked in.

Among them was Dori.

Dori

Among them was Jina.

Ryu

The two of them must have silently counted to a hundred. They must have recognised each other even from that distance and begun counting. Even after reaching one hundred – long enough to confirm the other wasn't a mirage that would dissolve – they continued staring, just to be certain. Perhaps they didn't dare step forward, afraid of shattering the illusion.

As if someone had pressed play, they moved towards each other and came together as one, touching and kissing as though they could heal each other's wounds with their mouths. Around them, dozens of emaciated people sprawled across the floor, their exhausted bodies propped against walls, hunched like crumpled pieces of paper. They all gazed upward at a medieval portrait of a saint hanging high beside three crosses, an instrument of execution that had become the symbol of salvation. Here, where every person had retreated into their own anguish – even the saint, Jesus, and the two crucified thieves – these two young women were the only ones turned towards each other, holding each other. 'Why are you here? How did you end up here?' they whispered, their faces pressed close. 'You should've gone farther. You should've gone somewhere far away.' When one spoke, the other echoed her. The words emerged from different bodies, but they were identical.

Someone cursed and spat at them.

I didn't understand the words, but their disgust was unmistakable.

Just then, a low cry reverberated from a corner of the cathedral. People shifted restlessly in their sleep. A gust of wind rang the bell. In the darkness, I found myself muttering. I repeated the same sentence like a prayer.

I wouldn't have survived if it had been just Haemin and me.

I felt protected by the connection between Dori and Jina, by Joy's innocent expression. With them, the atmosphere shifted. It became possible not to grow numb to murder, violence, humiliation and despair. I remembered that even surrounded by all this evil, another kind of world could exist. I could tell Haemin hopeful things. Jina hurried through her tasks to care for Dori, who had grown frail since I'd last seen her. We watched the soldiers who might harm Joy, becoming her voice and her ears. When Haemin had meltdowns wanting his dad, Jina would describe what his dad was doing at that moment and where he was, how much he missed Haemin and his mum, as though she had witnessed it herself. We gathered to share meals. There were hands to hold.

Still, each of us carried our own pain and regret.

I had no way of knowing whether Dan was alive or dead. The possibility of his death paralysed me. Why did I insist it didn't have to be love? If I couldn't bring myself to say I loved him, I should have said, 'Your life matters more to me than anything.' I should have said, 'I'm fine without hearing you say you love me. I need you.' With just that, Dan would have understood what I had failed to tell him. The truth I couldn't put into words. He would have recognised the unique pattern of all those days we'd shared. He would have held that close, and perhaps it could have kept him from walking into danger.

It was dawn. From somewhere nearby I heard a *boom*, then the ground shook. Before I could determine whether I was dreaming or awake, another explosion erupted. Everyone screamed and rushed to the cathedral doors, pushing and pounding. The doors were secured with a latch on the outside. The windows were also covered with sheet metal. The explosions continued, and the ground kept shaking. We heard tanks and lorries rolling past. We had to get the doors open. We had to break them down. We had to see what was happening. But the cathedral contained only the saint's portrait, crosses and us. The crosses and portrait hung beyond our reach. We pressed together against the doors. A machine gun rattled violently outside. Everyone stepped back from the doors. Just as we were preparing to try again, the doors suddenly swung open. Someone had removed the latch from outside. A man rushed in.

—Liza!

He kept calling out to Liza, his voice breaking with tears. Several guards lay collapsed behind him. Despite the tension in the air, the surrounding area looked more intact than I'd expected. The bomb probably hadn't landed directly in front of us. A column of fire rose with a roar from the east. People poured out of the cathedral and scattered in every direction at full speed.

—Let's just get to that apartment first.

Jina grabbed Haemin's hand. Dori and Joy ran ahead of us. I didn't hear any gunfire. Jina announced our next destination as we pressed ourselves against the wall. I heard bombs exploding one after another from the east. The horizon turned red; the ground shook. Jina looked around.

—Everyone must have gone to the trenches.

It was still dark. We needed to get as far away as possible before sunrise. But I kept glancing back, even as we darted between buildings. Jina said we had to follow the river upstream, that a worse hell waited to the south. I slowed my pace. She looked back at me.

—You kids go first.

I couldn't hesitate. This wasn't something to hesitate over.

—I have to go find my husband.

—He's probably on the frontlines.

—He's not the type to carry a gun. He must be doing labour. He's somewhere around here.

—Let's go somewhere safe first. We can think there.

—I have to find him now. Please. You go ahead.

—You don't even know where he is.

Dori spoke up.

—He might be in the gymnasium . . . I'm not sure though.

Jina looked at Dori in surprise.

—How do you know?

—The day we were taken. The men got off there first.

—Where is it? Do you think you can find it again?

Jina and Dori started running ahead. I worried I was putting these children in danger. The noise from the east had quieted somewhat. We used buildings as cover, then cut across a park filled with thin, scraggly trees. The air had a slightly green cast. Haemin, who had been half-running, half-pulled along by the hand, gradually slowed to a stop and looked up at the trembling sky.

—Haemin, come on.

I tugged at his hand.

—Mum.

Haemin pointed towards the southern sky. I thought it was a bird. A large eagle. A black eagle that feeds on human flesh.

—Plane.

He murmured as if talking in his sleep.

—Dad told me that planes . . .

Jina ran over and hoisted Haemin onto her back.

Dori and Joy each grabbed one of my arms.

A large transport plane and several fighter planes flew over us from the south.

We ran past small houses. Dori pointed to a large building. We quieted our footsteps and crouched behind a wall. Snow swirled in the wind. We crept towards the building. The door stood open. Bodies were scattered everywhere. There were soldiers among them. After looking around, Dori said Dan wasn't there. Where could I possibly find him? Where can I find you, my dear? If he were alive, he would be looking for us, too.

—I have to go back.

I had to. I had to find him before we were separated forever.

—No. It's too dangerous.

—I'll never see him again if I don't go now.

—What about Haemin? You can't take him back there with you.

Jina touched my face with her dry, cracked hands. Only then did I realise I was crying. Tears streamed down without a sound. Jina was crying too. My marriage was so predictable, it was precarious. That's why I hadn't given it enough attention. I hadn't properly committed myself to our love. If we separated like this, I'd regret it for the rest of my life. I didn't want to live with that regret.

Jina pulled me close and whispered against my shoulder.

—You have to survive first. You have to live if you want to see him.

Dori interjected again.

—. . . She can't just sit here waiting.

I felt Jina's grip tighten around my hand.

—She might die before she even gets to him.

—She knows the risks, and she's going anyway. Because there's something more important than living or dying,

Dori looked into my eyes. Her voice was the smallest and firmest among us. She was right. There was something more important.

—Please, come with us.

—You know, Jina, coming with us won't guarantee they'll make it. They have their own path, their own kind of miracle waiting.

Our own miracle. Did such a thing still exist? Maybe we each have a person – someone to remember as a proper noun, not in relation to something else. Some people join the road but pass by in an instant. Others appear as naturally as the landscape we notice after having grown numb to it. To experience our miracle, we must go find it ourselves. We can't yearn for it while drifting apart. Even if we were to be enslaved again, as long as I could be reunited with Dan and anticipate another escape . . . I drew Jina into a hug, stroking her back. I promised to survive. My other miracle – busy growing even in this moment and unable to peel his eyes off the eastern sky – took the first step.

—Please survive. Please.

Jina.

—I'll think of you every day.

Dori.

None of us could promise to meet again.

The sun was hidden in the snow flurries, but the road was bright enough for them to distinguish the dangers from whatever good fortune lay ahead. They raced between trees reaching for the sky and looked back only once. As they claimed their miracle and charged towards an elsewhere, Dori, Jina and their small angel grew farther and farther away from me and Haemin.

Epilogue

Joy

I never told anyone, but I still remember the dream I had the night I lost sound. I flew. The world I saw from up there was tiny and beautiful. Everyone's heads turned into yellow, white, black dots. I no longer saw people, houses and trees – just mountains and rivers, fields and oceans. All these colours and brilliant lights. I got smaller as my view got bigger. The world shrank and shrank while the sky grew huge. Flying in the sky felt like diving in the ocean. There's no sound way up high or way down deep. Sounds just disappear. After that night, my world became more like space than Earth. There's no sound in outer space, and it's perfect even without it. I dreamt I flew so high I became an astronaut. That's why I lost sound.

I never told anyone, but I still remember the song. *Last night in a dream, I put on my flying wings and soared above the clouds. Daddy looks for me when I'm playing at Rainbow Park.* I sing it to myself every day. I know I'll forget it eventually. Everything about the song will get wiped clean from my memory. Until then, I'll learn the song of light. Light is as infinite as sound. It changes through all kinds of collaborations. Different pitches and depths and widths of light play off each other, making beautiful melodies and rhythms. I watch this fantastic performance several times a day. I want to tell Dori about it, but there's no way to explain it. It's like explaining sound to someone who can't hear.

I never told anyone, but I had other dreams too. I planned to become a poet, so I read the dictionary every day. I wanted to know loads and loads of words. The more words I learnt, the bigger my view got, like looking down from the sky. I also planned to become a novelist. I already picked a name for the main character of my first book: Wish. Such a pretty word. The main character of my second book will be named Hsiw. Wish has to exist for Hsiw to exist. I planned to become a painter too. I can see light performing, and drawing is just writing down its sheet music. I wanted to be a choreographer who dances without music. And a drummer – I wanted to play at least one musical instrument. I'm a dreamer. All these dreams wore me out, but I could dream about anything because I was young. I thought nobody could mess with my dreams and I couldn't mess with theirs, but my dreams hurt my parents. Every single dream made them unhappy. When I wrote a poem, they'd compliment me but whisper, 'If only she hadn't lost her hearing.' When I drew something, they'd pat me on the back but mutter, 'If only we had more money.' When I danced, they'd tell me I looked pretty and hug me in a way that made me sad. So I didn't want to do any of it anymore – writing, painting, dancing. When only Dori and I were left, I started dreaming a new dream: to become an adult. An adult who doesn't have to hide behind her big sister. I got scared whenever Dori hid me or covered my eyes. That was way scarier than keeping my eyes wide open and seeing everything. I wanted to tell her to stop, to please quit getting in my way. But if I didn't hide, if I saw everything, Dori would fall apart. She'd panic and forget to protect herself. I had to be invisible for Dori to fight her hardest. So I changed how I thought about it. Whenever Dori stepped in front of me, we were joining forces. We got stronger together, like Transformers. Eventually, I felt like we were combining powers just by holding hands. I wanted to become an adult already so I could fight my own fights without Dori. But first, I had to grow tall and learn lots of things. Like what love is.

Love . . . I have so much to say about love. Stupid adults think I don't know anything, but I could draw a chart of everyone we spent time with and put arrows showing who loved who. Poor Geonji. If he loved me instead of Jina, no one would be sad. Geonji treated me like a puppy and sometimes really seemed to think of me as one. He'd say whatever popped into his head as he would in front of a puppy, probably thinking I couldn't understand. But I can see past sound as long as I can read people's lips and faces. I can see that Geonji has a red gem stuck in his heart. It'll keep giving him strength like a battery that never dies. He'll walk to the end of the Earth with that gem's power. As someone who once dreamt of being an artist, I know love doesn't have conclusions. Even if you tie a nice bow for the sake of an ending, a bow's just a bow. The story keeps going after the bow. You can't stop that. There's no bow on Geonji's love. There's no bow on mine either.

Every time Dori got hurt, I took a big step towards becoming an adult.

I learnt how to tell important things from unimportant ones.

But in the end, I didn't get to become an adult.

The night I lost sound, I dreamt of flying in the sky. I soared and soared without falling, then became an astronaut. Years before, I'd had a scary dream about falling and woke up crying. Dad patted my back and said the dream was helping me grow taller. I should've had more of those falling dreams and become an adult . . . But I just kept flying, too scared to fall. The night I took my last breath, I dreamt of flying across space, which is the same as flying across time. I soared and soared across time and saw what's beyond this place. Then I couldn't open my eyes.

There are so many memories and thoughts I never told anyone. I practised cutting them down to very short sentences so I wouldn't forget. Long, wandering stories got shorter like life itself, until they became a single word stuck in my heart. There's a gem inside me too, and it shines blue. Just like I could see what was inside Geonji's heart, Dori must've noticed what was inside mine. My promise, my gem, will never ever change.

Geonji

It looked like a tree, but I couldn't accept it as one.

I didn't know its name for the longest time.

Still, I ate its fruits, leaned against its massive trunk, carved my memories into its bark.

Then one day I figured it out.

That word *baobab* I kept hearing people say – turns out it meant this tree.

Now I call the baobab by its name.

Some things, you just come to know.

I walked and ran for so long I lost track of time. Ran into danger everywhere. Got swept up in a war before I even knew it was war. I killed people without knowing what was happening. Surviving without killing . . . was that possible? Did anyone manage that? I don't know. The world flipped upside down. All order was gone.

Was there any honour left in life?

Was murder still evil?

I hid among corpses, barely escaping death myself. Heard

massive explosions from places I'd just fled. The fever and migraines got so bad I carved into my skin, trying to kill one pain with another. Got captured by those bastards, became their plaything. Ate bugs off the ground when there was nothing else. Through all of it, one thought: *I can't die like this. This can't end like this.*

When I jolt awake in the dark, quiet night, those sensations come back like bandits. I sink into a rotten shame and guilt, unable to fall back asleep, barely fighting off the urge to die.

People live here. A very small number. We live only as nature allows. We avoid conflict and look after each other with careful distance. We swim and fish every day, eat fruits and scatter the seeds. Our lives are neither abundant nor lacking. Humans didn't go extinct, but that day might still come. I don't know how big the world is. I don't even know where I am. I don't know what's happening on the other side of this continent, whether people are still killing each other.

There's a delay between experience and understanding. There was something I hadn't realised, even as I killed and escaped and hid and ran during the war, even as I walked and walked until my mind went completely blank. I just knew I loved Jina. Nothing else mattered. That's how I got here, how I learnt to stay in one place. Each morning began with a mantra: *Stop thinking about death. Just wait it out.* I lived thousands of days like that, and then some.

It was a sunny summer day. I took a dugout canoe to a nearby beach, cast a net, then got swept up in a wave and flipped over. While pulling myself back on, I realised something.

Jina loved Dori.

I couldn't get back on. The canoe flipped again. I treaded water, thinking. Not upset, just embarrassed. If Jina could see me now and hear what I was thinking, she'd bust up laughing. The net floated away, but the canoe bobbed nearby.

So what. Doesn't change anything.

I watched the net drift farther away. What I was waiting for wasn't Jina's love, and she'd be waiting for me whether she loved me back or not. I climbed back in the canoe, staring at the horizon. I curled up and bit my tongue, then finally let out this tiny whisper.

—I miss you.

I still remember everything. Jina's face, her voice, her laugh, her red hair. I missed her so much I burst into tears. I cried until I couldn't breathe and my heart ached. I'd held it in, this overwhelming feeling. Afraid it would destroy me, I'd stopped myself from even thinking about missing her. I was sobbing and smacking myself in the head when this terrifying thought hit me and I sat up. What if I suddenly realise that Jina's no longer alive? That no matter how long I wait, I'll never see her again? What if I just know this one day? The fishing net I thought had drifted away was floating right by the canoe. I rinsed my face in the ocean and looked at the shore. If I had to make one decision in life, I'd choose Kwon Jina every time. No matter how bad things got, I could always keep going if it would lead me to her. I still have this dream that hasn't come true yet. I want to catch fish, pick sweet berries and give them to someone I love. I'll keep living, endlessly praying she's alive. Please. That's all I ask.

Us

—Dori.

—Yeah?

—Do you know how old the Earth is?

— . . . I used to.

—It's 4.5 billion years old. The universe, 15 billion. And they say humans have been around for about 2 billion.

—I can't believe you remember all that.

—I just made it up.

—What!

—Hey, remember I told you about having prophetic dreams?

—You said that was a joke!

—It's not, though. I only said it was a joke in case you couldn't handle it.

—Uh-huh.

—I actually dreamt that we met again. Even before I saw you at the cathedral.

—I've had dreams like that.

— . . .

— . . . Does that mean I have prophetic dreams, too?

—Anyway. I have this recurring dream, and it's about the end of humanity.

— . . . How often do you have it?

—About once a year. It's incredibly vivid.

—The end of humanity?

—Yeah. Humans die out, and only animals and plants survive. But humans don't realise they're dead and live on as ghosts. Like *The Sixth Sense.* You've seen it, right?

—Yeah.

—Everyone's a ghost like Dr Malcolm, so there's no one to tell them, 'Hey, you're a ghost.' And no one dies since they're all ghosts already. Another ice age comes, all the animals and plants die out, then everything thaws and different life forms emerge. The Earth creates and destroys and creates all sorts of things for billions of years. Meanwhile, humans continue existing as ghosts. Not realising what they are, worrying about the environment and the future of humanity.

— . . .

—Scary, huh?

—So are humans going extinct?

—I keep thinking about that too. Can we really call it extinction if we stay ghosts forever?

—No, I'm asking, are humans about to go extinct?

—Hmm . . . Even if it doesn't happen right away, eventually?

—Well, that's one hell of a dream.

—Yeah. I wake up exhausted. A bit drowsy and . . . I get this weird feeling.

—Weird feeling?

—I start wondering if *I'm* a ghost. If I'm living without realising that the world's already screwed.

— . . . What do you mean, screwed?

—I've come to the conclusion that we're not really screwed as long as we *know* we're screwed.

—When are we really screwed, then?

—When we don't even know it.

— . . . Like ghosts?

—Yeah. You can't get more screwed than ghosts.

—I don't think I get it.

—Don't you think we'll know when that moment comes? We'll feel that it's all over.

—I used to always feel like death was right in front of me.

—Is it still there?

—I don't think about it anymore.

— . . .

—Maybe I'm a ghost.

—You're human for sure. A human so cute and smart and pretty, I can't take my eyes off you.

—You know, I saw Geonji not too long ago.

—Geonji?

—Yeah. An older Geonji. He's changed a lot, but I recognised him. In a dream, you just know.

—An older Geonji . . .

—He was alone on a bright, warm beach. He was sending a bottle into the ocean.

—He told you, too, huh?

—What?

—His dream.

—Never heard it. What was Geonji's dream?

—. . .

—. . .

—. . . Maybe she *does* have prophetic dreams.

—What?

—Nothing. So Geonji sent the bottle off?

—Yeah.

—Why?

—I don't know. I just remember him doing that. I woke up and instantly forgot everything else that happened.

—. . .

—Do you think we can all meet again?

—. . . Someday, as long as we remember and wish.

—. . .

—. . .

—Should we head out?

—Yeah. Let's get up.

—Jina.

—Yeah?

—I love you.

Author's note

I return to the café where I'd often stop to read over my work. It was cold then. I'd sit there bundled up in three or four layers. Now there's nothing left for me to read, and outside, people walk by in summer clothes. I sit dazed, listening to music, when 'Ma rendi pur contento' comes up on my playlist and brings me back to myself.

It feels like I've circled around and around, only to find myself near where I used to be. Only the sense of it remains; I'm not who I was then, and you're not here. There was a time when I forgot myself and focused solely on your happiness. I could live that way again. If life is not unfolding but whole, nothing can be learned 'too late' – I knew that without needing to be told. And yet, so many things I thought unknowable were not so because you were silent, but because I did not listen or look. I truly hope that you are happy.

This was a story that needed to be written in one long breath. I wanted to give it a name, call it by its proper name. I wanted to take a precious, unmistakable fragment of memory – one where I could be myself – and make it tangible.

There are parts I left unexplained. They're fine left blank, maybe even better when readers can imagine for themselves. As with anything, writing is lonely work. I wanted to step aside from time to time and create a space for readers to join me.

Even on the day humanity perishes and everything we've made turns to ash, people will love. You, and we, will love. The many words of love left behind will wander the silent Earth like ghosts, like wind. Love will remain. Even as everything vanishes, love will be, like the universe.

Summer 2017
Choi Jin-young

Translator's interview with the author

This interview with Choi Jin-young, conducted in Korean and translated by Soje, originally appeared in Words Without Borders: The Queer Issue IX, *June 2018.*

In your author's note, you wrote, 'This was a story that had to be written in one long breath.' What made *Everything Happened at Once* different from the others?

Though I'd written about lesbians in several short stories and novels, I'd never put them front and centre. The lesbian couples in my novels never got the chance to properly love, either. Suseon from *The Never-Ending Song* is a lesbian, but that novel is about three generations of women, so it was hard to focus only on her love life. Suseon is from my mother's generation. Our generation of queers experiences much oppression and discrimination, so you can only imagine what it was like for the generation before us. Homosexuality must've been nearly impossible to even mention. So I couldn't make that novel about a lesbian romance, but I did want to write a whole novel centered on a lesbian couple before I retired.

You're too young to be talking about retirement!

I'm always thinking about retirement. [*laughs*] I'm always thinking, *This could be my last novel.*

I saw that you did a talk last fall with Kim Hye-jin, the author of *Concerning My Daughter*. It's a very different novel from yours, but it invites comparison since you're both writing about queer women. How do you feel about that?

Our books came out around the same time, as part of [Korean publisher] Minumsa's Young Author Series, and since our subjects were similar, the publisher had us do a promotional event together. I felt very encouraged. There's a lesbian couple in Kim Hye-jin's novel too, but as you said, they feel quite different. I focused mainly on the love story, while *Concerning My Daughter* almost feels like a survival guide for lesbian couples in Korea.

What really stuck with me from that novel was their house [shared by the mother, the daughter and her partner] and that feeling of being trapped. In your book, there's barren land—

I just send them to Russia. [*laughs*]

But they can both be categorised as queer fiction.

Yes. And I really welcome it – the fact that there's another young woman writing at the same time, that I can converse with her, and that there are readers interested in us. I gain strength from it. If we lived in a time when these things couldn't be discussed, I don't think my novel could've received this much love. Queers and women still lack many rights, but at least these issues are part of the conversation now. When *The Never-Ending Song* came out in 2011, no one really paid attention to its queer themes. Instead, I kept getting asked 'Why don't you write stories with male narrators?' and 'Why do you only write about women?' My first book was about a teenage girl, my second book was about three generations of women, and I have many short stories with female narrators.

But they don't ask male authors that.

That's why it's a strange question. 'Why do you only write female protagonists?' I heard it so often that I grew self-conscious. 'Do I need to write more men?' [*laughs*] Because there are no 'proper' men in my novels. They always cause trouble in some way . . .

One of the defining features of *Everything Happened at Once* is its multiple narrators. Dori and Jina speak for themselves as queer women, which contrasts with *Concerning My Daughter*, where the heterosexual mother narrates in the first person. Why did you write in multiple first-person narration, rather than third-person omniscient?

To be completely honest, I'm just used to writing like that. If you look at my previous works, the main characters usually all speak in the first person, rather than a single narrator leading the story. I write to hear all of their stories. Instead of seeing them through someone else's distorted perspective, I'm giving the cast an equal chance to speak. I think this also heightens the reader's engagement.

I can think of an exception, but I'll keep it vague since it's a spoiler. When Dori and Jina reunite, they each narrate a sentence before the scene shifts to another character's perspective. Since the whole journey of their falling in love is told in the first person, the switch at this emotional climax comes unexpectedly. Voyeurism is often a problem in films about lesbians, but there is nothing like that here. I appreciated how the people around Dori and Jina never look at them that way.

I mean, I don't think I should write like that. [*laughs*] One of the things I set out to do while writing this novel was to make it happy. I'd written a lot of tragedies, and I felt deeply ashamed of that. The reality I saw around me didn't have a happy ending, so forcing my fiction to have one felt like a lie. Even mentioning hope felt deceptive. At the same time, I wondered, 'Why can't I write something different?' I felt guilty about dragging all my beloved characters to hell. So I was determined to keep them all alive – especially the characters people think could never survive in real life.

I can see traces of your usual concerns in each character's interiority, but ultimately the novel feels hopeful. I was reflecting on my own life while reading it!

Me too. One day I realised that thinking 'This could never happen in real life!' is itself a contradiction. I'm writing a novel – why do I keep getting caught up in reality? Can't I just write the story I want? Eventually, I realised that this approach works. I'm very grateful that readers find hope in *Everything Happened at Once*, and now I want to take it even further. I wish for society to change so that I'm not constantly asking myself as I write, 'Does this make sense?'

In past interviews, you've cited Christophe Bataille's *Annam* and Cormac McCarthy's *The Road* as inspirations for *Everything Happened at Once*.

Annam is about French missionaries in Vietnam. It unfolds in brief episodes, and the characters remain beautiful and noble even under miserable circumstances. As you turn the pages, drunk on the prose and the atmosphere, what remains is the love between two people you never expected to fall in love. I wanted to find that love – what you might call the core of the novel – in mine, too. From *The Road*, I borrowed what I needed for my own apocalyptic story. It's also about a father and son, and I was curious what would happen if the protagonists were women.

I found out that while the original title is *Annam*, the Korean translation is *The Unreachable Country*. What is the country that can't be reached?

It feels a little ironic. The missionaries are in Vietnam, a land completely unfamiliar to them. Maybe it's like Korea's Gochang County or Punggi-eup in Yeongju – places clearly marked on the map but that we've never heard of. I think love is similar. It feels unreachable, but it isn't. Everyone loves, but we all doubt and deny our own love. The protagonists in *Annam* begin as a priest and a nun who fall in love with each other. In their world, their physical relationship makes no sense, but what in love couldn't make sense? There's no such thing as a love that doesn't make sense. Priests can love; men can love men; women can love women; someone can love across gender without ever settling on a label; people with twenty- or thirty-year age differences can love each other. You can fall in love even the day before you die. But some people show extreme contempt for certain kinds of love, calling it senseless and trying to exclude it from the category of love. But that's all very unfair, isn't it?

Towards the beginning of the novel, Geonji admits to feeling 'relieved living like this . . . everyone equally screwed'. After getting to the story of his family situation before the disaster, I understood where he was coming from. But the novel eventually shows that this lawless environment isn't actually 'equally'

unfortunate. Women, for instance, are specifically targeted for certain crimes.

I've actually heard this sort of thing from teenagers. I worked briefly as a tutor, and these middle-school boys would get so stressed that they'd say, very earnestly, 'Man, a war needs to just start already.'

Why?

Oh, because they didn't want to take their test tomorrow. [*laughs*]

That's so extreme!

But I heard that in university too. People say that kind of thing when they're in pain – when they don't want tomorrow to come, can't see a future.

There's something else I recently remembered. Kang Ji-sook told me about her first short film, which has a Deaf protagonist. She explained that hearing people assume Deaf people wish they could hear. But some Deaf people probably wish for everyone in the world to be Deaf instead. I found this logic very convincing. If I'm already used to living in a silent world, I might prefer for everyone not to hear, rather than for me to suddenly start hearing . . .

These political conversations feel reflected in the male characters, especially when Jina tells her dad, 'Dad,

I'm already a dog here. A dog,' and he doesn't get what she means. As a cisgender heterosexual man, he talks about becoming 'the rulers of a new nation' and all that, without understanding why his own daughter might not want this. It all hits too close to home, what with the state of South Korean politics . . .

We're dying over here and they tell us to 'just put up with it', you know? They tell us it's getting much better, even as they ignore certain human rights, demanding our sacrifice in service of 'a world where we can all live well together' – a contradiction in itself. That's the voice of Jina's father.

The realism! The novel imagines a future Korea where everyone's in Russia, but you captured present-day Korean society so well.

Because I live in our current reality.

I've been wondering: Jina has red hair and grey eyes. Later in the novel, Dori asks why Jina's hair is red, but her question goes unanswered. Is it dyed? Is she not Korean?

I intended her to be mixed race. One of Jina's grandparents or ancestors was a foreigner, but I didn't explain that in the novel. You know, not a single person thinks it's weird for Jina and Dori to love each other. They just accept it. I wanted to do the same for mixed-race identity and disability.

The notion that these things require explanation seems absurd.

It's also set in a post-apocalyptic future. Who knows what demographic shifts would've occurred by then!

That's why I figured it was better not to explain myself. You don't need a reason 'why' Joy became Deaf, 'why' Jina is mixed race, 'why' a woman loves another woman. They're just people living their lives. Wouldn't explaining be even weirder?

This might be a strange question to end on, but I listened to 'Ma rendi pur contento' this morning. Do you have a favourite version?

As I wrote in my author's note, there's a lot I didn't include in the novel – what's said in sign language or who sings the version of 'Ma rendi pur contento' that Dori listens to, all those details. If I name the singer, people will go listen to that version, and that version will become the definitive song. I'd like everyone to have their own version. That way, the Dori and Jina in everyone's imaginations can be different.

About the author

CHOI JIN-YOUNG began writing twenty years ago. She is now one of Korea's foremost novelists, having amassed several prestigious prizes, including the Yi Sang Literary Award, Hankyoreh Literary Award and Shin Dong-yup Literary Prize.

Her record-breaking novella, *Hunger*, has sold 400,000 copies and been translated into 10 languages.

About the translator

SOJE is a poet and a translator from Korean living in New York. They have been listed for the National Translation Award in Poetry, the PEN Award for Poetry in Translation and the Sarah Maguire Prize for Poetry in Translation. In 2024, they served as the National Centre for Writing's Translator in Residence. Soje also makes *chogwa*, a zine featuring one Korean poem with multiple English translations.

This brazen book was created by

Publisher: Romilly Morgan
Junior Commissioning Editor: Jane Link
Creative Director: Mel Four
Senior Editor: Alex Stetter
Editorial Assistant: Emily Campbell
Typesetter: Six Red Marbles
Production Controller: Sarah Parry
Sales: Lucy Helliwell
Publicity & Marketing: Charlotte Sanders and Ailie Springall